David M'Laren

The Light of the World

David M'Laren

The Light of the World

ISBN/EAN: 9783337270582

Printed in Europe, USA, Canada, Australia, Japan

Cover: Foto ©Andreas Hilbeck / pixelio.de

More available books at **www.hansebooks.com**

THE
LIGHT OF THE WORLD

BY

DAVID M‘LAREN, M.A.

MINISTER OF HUMBIE

EDINBURGH: DAVID DOUGLAS

1878

CONTENTS.

CONTENTS.

I.

INTRODUCTORY.

THIS book is not intended to be polemical. It does not profess to offer a contribution to the great discussion concerning the Person of Christ, which has for some time been going on without having apparently as yet reached its final stage. With the larger problems which are beginning so profoundly to interest, and it may be to vex, the churches in this country, the writer is not unfamiliar, and he may hope in an indirect way to be helpful to some in the study even of them ; but their direct treatment he leaves meanwhile to other and abler hands.

Neither is this an exegetical treatise. Of critical interpretations of the recorded sayings of Jesus there is no lack. In the way of verbal criticism of the Gospels not much remains for a new gleaner. That work has been done,—as some think, overdone. The student is more likely to be embarrassed by the multitude of his counsellors and the discordancy of their counsel, than hindered by want of help ; and he may sometimes be tempted to think that orthodox and liberal alike have pored and quibbled and wrangled so long over the letter, that the spirit has been well-nigh quenched.   This is not a new commentary on the words of our Lord.

It will not venture to call itself an apology. Its design is to invite attention to the pure and undefiled doctrine of Jesus ; to point out some of its salient features which seem to be strangely neglected ; to vindicate its claim upon this bewildered generation ; to recommend anxious inquirers, amid the voices of the time, to "hear Him."

For, after all, the doctrine of Jesus Christ occupies a place of considerable importance in the world.   It is a great fact.   Whether John wrote the fourth Gospel or not, whether the others assumed their present shape in the first century of the Christian era or the second, by what process soever the discourses of Jesus assumed the form in which we now possess them, and whatever opinion be held on the subject of inspiration, we have—untouched by criticism, unspoiled by metaphysics—those precious frag-ments breathing a wisdom which is pure, peaceable, and fruitful of good works. It is more than doubtful whether we do them justice. On the one hand, the traditional theology, taking its stand on plenary inspiration and literal infallibility of the Scriptures, will not present the religion of Jesus unless in the dress of a fully developed philosophical scheme; on the other, criticism is throwing new light on the history of religion and the composition of the Bible, and science is shaking men's ancient conception of the supernatural, and the general conscience is rising in revolt against some of the prominent portions of the Augustinian system; and between the two, Christianity is losing its hold, not only on the mass but upon the intelligence of modern society. This may be denied; but those who know best the signs of the times know that it is true. We are being ruined by the falsehood of extremes. Our successors, we may hope, will profit by the clash and the conflict, and religion once more be a power in the land; but meanwhile we are tossed about by strange cross-currents of teaching, and many are perplexed, and some are in despair. Would it not be wise to go apart for a little to some quiet place, and listen to him who saith: " Come unto me, all ye that labour and are heavy laden, and I will give you rest. Take my yoke upon you and learn of me ; for I am meek and lowly in heart, and ye shall find rest unto your souls "?

There are two classes of readers whom, in especial, the present writer would be glad to address. Those, firstly, who are off the old moorings, and are drifting on a dark and troubled sea, who have dabbled in geology, and read Matthew Arnold, and been fascinated by the confident precision of Bain or the imposing breadth of Spencer,—young men, not flippant in thought or speech, not loose in conduct, in whose honest doubt I am sure there lives more faith than in half our bigoted believing,—healthy frank-hearted youths, who are dissatisfied with the creeds, and often find their spiritual pastors and masters blind guides, I would ask not too hastily to conclude, because Calvinism may be out of date, and the infallible Bible seems to be going the way of the infallible church, that there is nothing in the Christian religion worth their attention ; but to give a fair hearing to Jesus' own words, and see whether they do not commend themselves to their conscience, and supply some truth which may guide and cheer us in the battle of life, and give us comfort when we come to die.

To those, also, of every shade of opinion and form of worship, who have learned to cherish his words because they have found them to be spirit and life ; to all meek and quiet souls who love the Lord Jesus in sincerity, whether they repose in the calm of an untroubled faith or have conquered in the fight with doubt, are these chapters offered in brotherly sympathy.

II.

CAREER OF JESUS.

JESUS of Nazareth was first of all a Teacher.
This is his most obvious character, and that
which most certainly belongs to him.   He
believed himself, and was believed by some of
his contemporaries, to be the Messiah, the
anointed Deliverer of Israel.   To a later generation he was the eternal Son of God, the
Word made flesh, the ideal Head of humanity.
To fully developed theology he is both God
and man, in two distinct natures and one person
for ever.   In the case of many who receive this
dogma, the divinity not unnaturally swallows up
the humanity.   The tendency of modern thought
is to exhibit more plainly his human nature
and realise his place in history, with the effect,
in the meantime, of throwing his Godhead
into the background.   And it must be confessed
that there is a large number of persons for

whom he is neither God nor man, but a phantasm, mysterious and unrealised.

The fact is that he was a Jewish rabbi, or rather a prophet among the rabbis of his day. In the reign of Tiberius Cæsar, Pontius Pilate being governor of Judæa, Herod tetrarch of Galilee, Annas and Caiaphas holding a joint or alternate high priesthood, he began to teach and to preach. He was about thirty years of age. His youth had been passed in an obscure Galilean town, and he had worked at a carpenter's bench, being probably the chief support of his mother and younger brothers. He had no systematic training, no diploma of academic distinction, no ecclesiastical license. There was not even that association with some sect or school, that relation of discipleship to a teacher of repute, which was the recognised introduction to the career of a teacher of the Law. He sat at the feet of no rabbi. He came not forth from the company of the Essenes. All the research and ingenuity of critics has failed to establish a consistent theory of his natural growth and culture, to affiliate him to any of his predecessors, to explain his indebtedness to the circumstances of his time. He drew no inspiration from the Talmud. Neither Hillel

nor Shammai can call him their son. His
relation to the spirit of his age is not one of
obligation but of opposition ; and the more we
learn to understand the thought, the life, the
various influences, political, social, religious, which
played around him, the fewer are the points of
contact we can discover, the more perplexing
as an historical problem does his appearing
become.

To one man only does he stand in any way
related ; and he, too, was one who was apart
from all the schools. From his simple preaching of repentance, Jesus, as a teacher, cannot be
said to have learned. To the great revivalist of
Jordan he paid the respect of receiving baptism
at his hands, he recognised him as his fore-
runner, and arraigned his countrymen for their
neglect of his message ; but he took an independent line, and expressly contrasted John's
method and position with his own.

He came forward of his own accord, by his
Father's command, and in his Father's name.
A few disciples gathered themselves around him,
chiefly fishermen from the towns on the Sea of
Galilee. A small company of women attached
themselves to him after a time. He preached
in the synagogues, he taught in the fields, on the

hills, in the streets, from a boat on Gennesaret, in the porch of the Temple. Wherever he found listeners he was ready to teach, to comfort, to reprove, to proclaim the good news of the kingdom of God. Assuming from the first an attitude of hostility to the dominant sects, and especially to the Pharisees, the most powerful of all, by his superiority in argument and his unsparing exposure of their inner corruption, he soon excited a relentless hatred among the influential classes, and fell a victim, after not more than three years of public work, to their bigotry and ill will.

Outwardly and humanly speaking, his ministry might be said to have met with little success. "He came unto his own, and his own received him not." His mother was perhaps his first disciple. His brethren were, at all events up to a late period of his life, open unbelievers. Not till after his ascension did they join the church, of which some of them became leading members. His neighbours and early acquaintances not only refused to believe in the carpenter's son, but when he appeared publicly in the synagogue of Nazareth, after listening a while with curious eagerness and involuntary admiration, they ended by seizing him in an access of fury, and trying to hurl him from the brow of their hill.   In Capernaum and the neighbouring parts of Galilee he met with more success.   Thence he drew the most faithful of his followers.   And if we receive St. Paul's statement that five hundred brethren saw him there after his resurrection, it will appear that his ministry had more fruit than we should infer from the narrative of the Gospels.   This, at all events, is His own verdict ; " Woe unto thee, Chorazin ! woe unto thee, Bethsaida ! for if the mighty works, which were done in you, had been done in Tyre and Sidon, they would have repented long ago in sackcloth and ashes.   But I say unto you, It shall be more tolerable for Tyre and Sidon at the day of judgment, than for you.   And thou, Capernaum, which art exalted unto heaven, shalt be brought down to hell : for if the mighty works which have been done in thee, had been done in Sodom, it would have remained until this day.   But I say unto you, It shall be more tolerable for Sodom at the day of judgment, than for thee."

In Jerusalem he had not many disciples. Nicodemus, a ruler, came to him, but secretly, for fear of the Jews ; and though he came forward with Joseph of Arimathæa to bury him, he never openly acknowledged him during his lifetime. None of the Pharisees or Chief Priests believed on him. On the whole, Jerusalem distinctly and with bloody emphasis rejected him. Its chief men hated him for denouncing their hypocrisy and assailing their authority. Its populace were willing enough to receive him if he would be a king after their heart, to chase out the Romans and restore the empire of David ; but they did not want to listen to sharp moral lectures and beautiful parables about a spiritual kingdom, and so they were easily persuaded to clamour for his blood. His final testimony concerning the capital is to be found in the twenty-third chapter of Matthew, with its scathing sentences of woe on the blind guides, the generation of vipers, and its incomparably pathetic close, in which his breaking heart laments over the city of God : " O Jerusalem, Jerusalem, thou that killest the prophets, and stonest them that are sent unto thee, how often would I have gathered thy children together, as a hen gathereth her chickens under her wings, and ye would not ! Behold, your house is left unto you desolate."

They seized him as a heretic, charged him with blasphemy, accused him before the governor as a disturber of the public peace, crucified him between two thieves, and mocked him as he hung. "And he said, 'It is finished,' and bowed his head and gave up the ghost."

III.

FORM AND MANNER.

OF this teaching, which has so largely influenced the world, we possess only fragments. He published no book. His words were not reported. No Baruch recorded the sayings of this prophet during his lifetime, and under his direction and revisal. At first handed down orally, there were gradually formed written collections, of which the original of our present Gospel of St. Matthew is the type; and a document appears to have acquired authority in the church generally as an authentic record, which formed the ground-work of our present Gospels of Matthew, Mark, and Luke. These took final shape somewhere in the latter half of the first century of our era. The Gospel of John represents another line of tradition. The whole question of its authorship and authenticity is now the subject of keen debate, and we wish to avoid, as far as may be, what is matter of controversy. Without assuming the absolute truth of the theory of apostolic authorship, it may suffice to express a conviction which need not too greatly tax even sceptical readers, that in that work we possess valuable records of undoubtedly authentic utterances of Jesus, however modified and coloured by the writer's peculiar cast of thought and style.

Thus have the precious fragments come down to us, consisting of regular discourses and of parables—a favourite and characteristic form—of discussion with inquirers and with adversaries, of casual remarks, of private conversations, a general acquaintance with which may safely be assumed.

Of the teacher's personal appearance, voice, and manner, all that which has so much to do with the effect of oral instruction, we have nothing to say. Nothing is recorded, no hint is given ; and, reverence apart, good taste forbids the indulgence of curious and fanciful remark. Perhaps it is expedient for us that we cannot know him after the flesh at all. But from the records we can judge of the simplicity, the limpid clearness, the incisiveness, the power, the charm of his utterance. He possessed that first requisite of a teacher of the people—a popular style. The phrase may have to many an evil sound ; for we are too much accustomed to a popularity which is gained by the use of strong and flowery language, by tawdry rhetoric and tricks of style, by loudness and bombast. But though by such means it is possible to gain the applause of the hour, no reputation thus acquired either spreads widely or endures long ; and above and beyond such noisy and ephemeral popularity is that which is accorded only to great men and a true style, to preachers like Martin Luther, to authors like John Bunyan, to poets like Robert Burns, to speakers like John Bright.   In this sense, with a popularity deep and abiding, confirmed by the use of eighteen centuries, and freely allowed by the strictest criticism, are our Lord's discourses popular, exercising over all men and in all languages an undisputed charm.

Occasionally, as if to strike dull ears and stir sluggish minds, his sayings are almost paradoxical ; and sometimes metaphor is used as a veil for things too high or too hard for his hearers to understand.   But, in general, his language is perfectly simple, and his images are drawn from common sights and sounds.   His words are always true to nature, and full of life.   The common people heard him gladly.   Officers of the scribes and Pharisees sent to arrest him were kept from laying hands on him by the fascination of his speech. "Never man," said they, "spake like this man." Many besides his townsmen of Nazareth must have "wondered at the gracious words which proceeded out of his mouth." And though we have them only in fragments, and read these in the strange dress of a western language, still is their beauty owned by minds of finest culture, and felt by the humble and unlearned.

IV.

METHOD.

NOTHING can be simpler than his method. He claimed to speak the word of his Father, and he sought for the proof and verification of what he said in the natural instincts, the conscience, the life of his brethren. This assertion may seem startling to those who cannot distinguish between the method of Jesus and that of his mediæval and modern followers. These have presented truth in the form of a mysterious system, to be accepted because it is vouched for by an infallible, that is, miraculously enlightened church, or because it is attested by certain evidence of a miraculous kind. The truth itself has been changed in their hands, theology has become the most abstruse of all sciences, the most difficult, and not the least dry of studies. The sweet word of Jesus has been forced into alliance with a crabbed philosophy. It takes a long and careful education even to understand its cardinal doctrines, let alone judging of their truth. So that unless the reader will remember that I am speaking not of the Pope or Dr. Paley, of schoolmen mediæval or modern, but of the teaching of Jesus himself, as exhibited in the Gospels, he may be surprised to hear that our Lord adopted a method so startlingly, if not dangerously, simple. But if he will bear this in mind, and consult his New Testament for himself, perhaps he will find that there is something in what I say. It is a fact that he communicated his greatest lessons to fishermen and publicans, to the Samaritan woman at Jacob's well, to the multitudes of Galilee. His arguments are such as require for their appreciation not learning, not subtlety, but common sense and rightness of feeling. They appeal to the common understanding, go straight to the heart of man, and challenge the witness which in its best feelings is found to the truth of God.

A few examples will serve better than assertion or disquisition.

Look at his treatment of the question of Sabbath observance. In his day that had become, as strangely enough the Sunday question among his own followers has become again, a matter of bigotry, a burden, a question of ancient precepts and traditions of men. Note with what freedom and boldness he handles the matter, how he sweeps away the quibbles of the Pharisees and the traditions of the elders, and brings the whole thing to the test of the law written on man's hearts by such plain questions as these, " Which of you shall have an ox or an ass fallen into a pit, and will not straightway pull him out on the Sabbath day ? Is it lawful to do good on the Sabbath day or to do evil ?" One likes to think of the face of a Scribe as he heard that. A common man's conduct towards his cattle called in to decide a question of divine law! the instincts of the human heart set above the traditions of the elders! One can judge of the effect by applying the same method in presence of Christian Pharisees to some dogmas of the Christian religion ; to the same Sabbath question itself for instance. But we digress. That is one example of the method of Jesus.

Here is another. If there is a more knotty and troublesome subject than the Sabbath it is prayer; as we of this generation well know. This is his way of treating the subject of prayer: "What man is there of you, who, if his son ask bread, will give him a stone ? If ye then, being evil, know how to give good gifts unto your children : how much more shall your Father which is in heaven give good gifts to them that ask him." God is our Father ; and if even an earthly father can be entreated with assurance by his child, how much more an heavenly ? The subject is taken out of the sphere of logic with its difficulties so familiar to us all, into that of life and love. Prayer becomes not a questionable expedient for influencing a deity seated apart in unapproachable majesty, not a means of imposing our will upon him and disturbing his plans, not a formal petition addressed to a great potentate : it is the pouring out, spontaneous and inevitable, of a child's penitence, trust, desire, into a heavenly Father's ear.

The question of pardon and reconciliation with God is a central one in the Christian as in all religions. With it all rites and sacrifices are concerned. In old times they sought to propitiate the offended deity by the blood of bulls and goats, by tithes and offerings, fastings and prayers. They bowed their heads as a bulrush, and put ashes on their hair. " They gave their first-born for their transgression, the fruit of their body for the sin of their soul." In later times they did penance, and made pilgrimages, and bought masses, and bequeathed lands to mother church. Among ourselves the favourite method of late has been to master a certain theory of atonement and go through certain peculiar but well-marked emotional experiences. What theories of atonement have become need not be told. Two are commonly received. The first and best boldly represents the death of Christ as a sacrifice in the plain old sense, by which the wrath of God is appeased, and heavenly blessing procured for a small number of favoured individuals. The other—I have no wish to caricature or offend—represents it as a subtle device for enabling God to show mercy to His favourites without doing violence to His justice.

It is instructive to compare this with the fifteenth of Luke. " What man of you having an hundred sheep ?" " Either what woman having ten pieces of silver ?" " Likewise"—not be it noted, " also" but—likewise, in the same way, " there is joy in heaven over one sinner that repenteth, more than over ninety and nine just persons that need no repentance." " This my son was dead, and is alive again ; and was lost, and is found."

For centuries before his time Jews and Samaritans had been discussing the rival claims of Jerusalem and Gerizim. It was a vital question in which place God should be worshipped. How does He treat it? Simply puts it aside, shows that worship turns not on place but on spirit. "God is a spirit, and they that worship Him must worship him in spirit and in truth."

The Pharisees were very particular about fasting and tithes, and outward observance of all kinds; very careful, as he said, to make clean the outside of the cup; very fond of imposing such burdens upon the people. "Two men," he said, "went up into the temple to pray, the one a Pharisee, the other a Publican." We know what the Pharisee had to boast of in the way of prayers, fasts, and offerings. The Publican, in all probability, had never once fasted in the course of his life, at least of his own will, and his prayers had not been much to speak of, but he stood afar off, and smote on his breast, saying, "God be merciful to me a sinner." "I tell you this man went down to his house justified rather than the other." What a mass of ecclesiastical pretensions and ritualistic ordinance that one sentence cuts sheer away!

To a certain extent this characteristic of the Lord's method was impressed upon it by the fact of his teaching being, in its historical connections, a reaction against the dead literalism and hypocritical formalism of the religious teaching current in Israel in his day. He was a reformer to whose boldness it is not easy for us to do justice ; a heretic, the frightfulness of whose heresy in the ears of the Scribes we can hardly understand. To be fair both to them and to him, this must be taken into account : that he innovated upon established beliefs more than Luther and Knox upon the papal system ; that he seemed to the religious leaders of the time to assail the very foundation of the faith, to despise what was most sacred, to blaspheme God. And this extreme position helped to bring out and emphasise that simple method of heart teaching, that recourse to the individual con-science, as Mr. Arnold excellently puts it, to which I seek to call attention. But it is the method of all great teachers; and, if you think of it, the only effectual method of really establishing spiritual truth and influencing spiritual life. It was the method of the prophets. One of the greatest of them lays down the principle clearly. "This commandment, which I command thee this day, it is not hidden from thee, neither is it far off. It is not in heaven that thou shouldest say, Who shall go up for us to heaven, and bring it unto us, that we may hear it and do it? Neither is it beyond the sea, that thou shouldest say, Who shall go over the sea for us, and bring it unto us, that we may hear it and do it? But the word is very nigh unto thee, in thy mouth, and in thy heart, that thou mayest do it." It was the method of Paul, who cites the foregoing, and condenses its truth in the phrase, "With the heart man believeth unto righteousness," and speaks of himself as commending truth to every man's conscience in the sight of God. But more conspicuously and more consistently than by any prophet or teacher was this method followed by the greatest Teacher of all. None ever spake with so simple and intense consciousness of the truth of his words; none ever relied so exclusively on the authority of his message, the power of the truth itself; none dispensed to such extent with argument or evidences, or appealed so confidently to the witness of the heart and conscience of men.

Really and ultimately there is no other way. Evidences of Christianity are very well in their place; but their place is that of apology and defence. And it is high time that the apologetics of Paley and Butler, so useful in their generation, should give way to a system more suited to the difficulties and the attacks of our day. But it must be remembered that at most apology can only secure a hearing for Christianity, and that he alone is a true disciple to whom its truth shines by its own light, and comes home in its own power. It is not what we say we believe, or make believe that we believe, or think we believe, that can save; but only that which we receive in cordial faith and love, and hide in our very heart. It is because he is assured that his word is true, being not his own but the Father's that sent him, because he knows what is in man, and judges that it must find a response in every honest heart, that his tone as a teacher is so high. He taught with authority and not as the Scribes; not with the authority of texts and traditions, the authority of dogma, demanding unthinking and unquestioning submission, but with the authority of one who was in the light of God, and saw light clearly, and had unbounded confidence in the truth which he spake. He believed that his word did touch the conscience of his hearers, and could not be rejected without conscious sin, and therefore he told the rulers of the Jews that that word itself would judge them at the last day.

And now it may be called rationalistic, and loose, and vague, and broad, and a great many hard names ; but it must be said that if we wish to be true to Christ, we must have his faith in the truth, his fearlessness, his simplicity. We must not expect men to receive our words because we put on gown or surplice and go up into pulpits, we must not think to do them good by means of unintelligible propositions. No food, natural or spiritual, is of use unless and until it is digested and assimilated. No truth is of any effect except on him to whom it is true. On this principle rests the method of Jesus. Inasmuch as the principle is absolute, his method is permanently and universally admirable. A faithful and fearless use of it was perhaps since his departure never more wanted than at this day.

V.

MIRACLES.

THE miracles of Jesus do not directly concern us in the present inquiry. We shall not be required to discuss their credibility, certainly not to argue as to their *à priori* possibility. They are only remotely and indirectly connected with our subject, and this relation needs only to be briefly indicated here.

They are commonly treated (1) as supplying the evidences necessary to establish our Lord's claim to be heard as a teacher sent from God ; (2) as in their own nature possessing a didactic or illustrative value.

1. To the contemporaries of Jesus, and perhaps in a still greater degree to the generation following, miracles seemed to be the appropriate voucher of a divine commission. " Show us a sign and we will believe." " Thou art a teacher sent from God : for no man can do the miracles which thou doest, except God were

with him." " Herein is a marvellous thing, that ye know not from whence he is, and yet he hath opened mine eyes." These utterances in the mouth of persons of various standing and culture undoubtedly represent the opinion of the time.

That from the earliest period in the history of the church the ministry of Jesus was believed to have been attested by signs and wonders there is no doubt ; that he did many wonderful works, particularly in the way of healing, criticism, even of a somewhat advanced school, is disposed to allow ; that the fame of this helped greatly to further the spread of his doctrine in the world, no one can deny.

Nay, a time came when the miracles came to be regarded as the chief support of faith. Men were summoned to believe on Jesus, not because his word touched the conscience, and was felt to be spirit and life, but because he wielded superhuman power, and, as an heavenly teacher, claimed to have his doctrine received without question or verification, in pure and simple faith. Defenders of the faith relied on the argument from miracles and prophecy as their main stay. It is thus that most of us were taught ; and hence devout persons cling to the letter of Scripture, and are jealous of any free handling of the stories of Balaam's ass and Jonah's whale, because they regard them as bound up with the healing of blind Bartimæus, and the raising of Lazarus, and fancy that, should these narratives be found to be unhistorical, they must confess that their faith is vain.

We live in a different atmosphere. Miracles, instead of being flourished as an irresistible weapon of polemical divinity, have to be defended with jealous care, and sometimes with vehemence born of fear. They are not a help but a hindrance to the faith of many. Intelligent Christians rather accept them because they believe, than believe because Jesus wrought miracles. Whether this mood is temporary or lasting, and this conviction right or wrong, such appears to be the temper of the time ; and to a generation of which this is the temper we shall not greatly recommend the teaching of our Lord by resting its acceptance on existing accounts of his miraculous powers.

After what has been said in the preceding chapter, it will be apparent that, to the present writer, this is not matter of grave concern. The coercive power of external signs was not an essential part of the method of Jesus. That rests on other principles ; and whatever we may think of the value of a faith which reposes not on intellectual and moral conviction, but on mere wonder and blind submission, it is enough that the doctrine of Christ needs no such expedients to secure the faith of the world, but has the witness in itself, and finds its best proof in the hearts of the meek, its sufficient confirmation in the lives of those who strive to do God's will.

2. It has been the practice of the best expositors to use the Gospel miracles not evidentially only but also didactically, as integral parts, that is to say, of the revelation made by him in life as well as in word, parables in action showing forth the same righteous love which it was the aim of his preaching to declare. They are not mere wonders to make people stare. They are quite different from the imaginative wonders of heathen fable, and the ecclesiastical miracles of the type of St. Januarius and our Lady of Lourdes. The devil, it is said, tempted him to compel the allegiance of an astonished multitude by throwing himself down from the pinnacle of the temple, but he repelled the temptation. The Pharisees demanded a sign from heaven, but he refused to yield to the demand. His works were performed

in his Father's name, and under the leading of his Father's providence. There are a very few that present features of difficulty; in general they are in perfect harmony with the story of his life. They fit into the Evangelist's ideal. They are such works as it became the Son of the Everlasting Father to do. Men who saw them, —much more men like the blind man of the ninth chapter of the Gospel according to St. John, who felt them,—were led to know the true God and to trust him. Whatever may be thought of their value as proofs of a divine commission, there can be little doubt as to their fitness as illustrations of the beneficence and compassion of the Father, whose works he said they were, and as shadows of those spiritual benefits, sight, healing, cleansing, newness of life, which he promised to those who should come and learn of him.

VI.

PARABLES.

NO portion of the teaching of Jesus is more characteristic than his parables, none more popular, none more precious ; none, it may be added, has suffered more at the hands of his friends. In some respects the best thing that could happen in regard to their study would be that the mass of accumulated exposition should disappear, so that disciples might receive them as they were uttered, and ponder them without note or comment other than his own. Much that is beautiful and edifying would thus doubtless be lost, but, in consideration of the advantage gained by the removal of the results of a false method, the loss might almost be borne.

Most commentators seem to have approached their task under an impression that the parables are a series of profound enigmas ; a set of religious puzzles, carefully put together on some cunning plan, in which the smallest detail represents some part of a system of fully developed theology. Protests are to be met with occasionally, and there is something to be gathered from almost all schools of interpretation ; but on the whole there has been heaped up a mass of ingenious and dogmatical glosses under which the simple truth and beauty of the stories have for many been overwhelmed.

Take for instance one of the simplest of them all, the story of the neighbour going at midnight and by sheer importunity extracting a loan from his sleepy friend, by which, in a way a child can understand if you let him alone, the Lord Jesus teaches us to pray, and illustrates his argument,—" If ye then being evil know how to give good gifts, how much more shall your Father in heaven give the Holy Spirit to them that ask him." Instead of exhibiting the bearing of the story, and clearing up the only point which could possibly present a difficulty, by showing how God is not compared to the churlish friend, but rather contrasted with him, so that the argument is from the success of importunity in a bad case, to the hopefulness of prayer addressed to one who is more ready to give than we are to ask—instead of this, commentators have wasted their ingenuity in the discussion of such questions as, What do the loaves represent? or, Who are signified by the children in bed? The loaves are the Trinity; they are man's food and life, or faith, hope, and charity. The fish represents faith, the egg hope. The newly-arrived guest is the spirit of man, or, according to others, the heathen world. The host is the natural man, the children in bed are the angels or the saints already in glory. When one has had to wade through much of this sort of thing in studying this subject, it is positively refreshing to come upon a blunt remark which a Spanish commentator, who must have suffered much at the hands of the allegorical school, makes in his exposition of the parable of the "Prodigal Son,"—"If you ask me what the fatted calf means, it means a calf and nothing but a calf."

But, it may be said, are not the parables then mysteries, dark sayings which yield their meaning to the initiated alone? This opinion seems to be supported by certain words of Christ himself. Being asked by the disciples why he spake in parables, he said, " Because it is given to you to know the mysteries of the kingdom of heaven, but to them it is not given. For whosoever hath, to him shall be given, and he shall have more abundance : but whosoever hath not, from him shall be taken away even that he hath." (Matt. xiii. 12.) Does this mean that he deliberately sought to hide his truth from the multitudes, and mocked them with an empty show of instruction? No indeed. He spoke thus after he had delivered the parable of "The Sower." The people had heard it. Some of them perhaps wondered why he thought it meet to tell them things which they all knew so well; and failed to see any value, or even any meaning in his words. They not only did not understand the parable, but, which was worse, they did not much care whether they understood it or not. The disciples too heard it, and neither did they understand ; but they believed that it was worth understanding, and asked the master to explain. Their eyes were blessed, for they saw that there was something to learn, and their ears because they were willing to hear. Bearing this in mind and making allowance for the fragmentary and condensed form of the remark, we judge that Christ's chief purpose was to enforce the salutary warning, "take heed how ye hear." Good hearing is in its way as important as good preaching, and for disciples everything practically depends on the way in which we receive the word. That which is to the pure in heart an illustration, is to the hardened a veil. The universe of God, to the spiritually-minded vocal of his glory, distracts the thoughts of the carnal from him ; and the gospel itself, the good news of God, is, according to St. Paul, a savour of life to them that believe, but a savour of death to them that perish.

Moreover, if the parables be dark sayings in that sense, they will not become light by elaborate trifling with mere details, but by a docile study of their scope and spirit. Our Lord's own exposition of the " Sower " and the " Tares " is the true model to be followed in all other cases ; and in fact, when we follow this method there is no great mystery about them. There are two parables which even thus read do present difficulties ; that of the " Unjust Steward," and that of the " Labourers in the Vineyard." In the former of these, a good deal of the difficulty commonly encountered arises from ambiguity in the English version, and disappears when it is pointed out that it was not the Lord Jesus, but the steward's employer that commended his guilty cleverness, and that we are exhorted to make friends not of, but with, or by means of the mammon of unrighteousness. Any attentive reader who notes these points can see that the story teaches that even from sinners saints may have something to learn ; that foresight and care are useful in spiritual matters as well as in the affairs of this world ; and that the best use to make of earthly riches is to spend them so that we shall have some grateful friends to speak for us on high.

In the other case the difficulties spring chiefly from two causes ; first, that same habit of trifling over details spoken of above, and secondly, the mistake of treating the parable as a separate enigma, instead of reading it along with the very significant conversation recorded immediately before, a mistake to which the division into chapters in our version lends itself. We must observe that the disciples had been asking the master what they should receive for forsaking all and following him, and that while assuring them of reward, and forbearing to notice directly the ungraciousness of re-minding him of their self-sacrifice and asking its price, he intimated to them that many who should hereafter be called might be before them, and that if they harboured sentiments so greatly at variance with the spirit of his service, they might even fail after all. If the parable is read with all this in our mind, we understand how it teaches that the rewards of the kingdom are of grace and not of debt, and exposes the folly and unloveliness of envying and grieving at the good of other men.

These two excepted, I do not know that there is one of our Lord's parables that cannot be understood by all who are willing to learn. Does any man with a heart in his bosom want a " master of sentences " to unfold the message of the "Good Samaritan," or the "Prodigal Son?" Preachers may draw out their meaning, and enforce their lessons—and if they do so in a right spirit they can hardly be better employed ; but let them beware that they do not create difficulty where difficulty is none, and darken what is plain by laboured or fanciful explanation. On the whole, one endorses the remark of a reviewer in one of our newspapers : " It would be well if divines of all schools would let the parables alone, and allow people to read them for themselves, without note or comment. Readings, whether new or old, of these simple and instructive stories, are merely an impertinence."

VII.

JUDAISM.

IT has been remarked already that Jesus occupied a position of pronounced hostility to the religion of his time ; and was regarded by the leaders of his people as a heretic of the most dangerous kind.

There were three great parties in the religious world—Pharisees, Sadducees, and Essenes.

The last-named scarcely, if at all, appear in the sacred records, and need not detain us long. Of their creed little is known, and as their practice consisted in a rigid asceticism in which they held themselves aloof from the life of the people, and cultivated a private and peculiar discipline, their influence upon the national religion was of minor importance. John the Baptist had some affinity with them ; but Jesus had little or none, and even offers in most points a marked contrast to their system. He indeed, like them, insisted on purity of life ; but it was in a far different way. Their holiness was only negative; his was of a positive and useful kind. They fled from temptation, his plan was to meet and overcome it. They despised the body; he honoured and cherished it. They shunned the converse of men; he mingled freely with his fellows. They aimed at making themselves dead to the world; he died for it. They dreaded God and tried to propitiate him by self-torture; he trusted God and taught that he is to be pleased by service and self-sacrifice. Their discipline tended to selfish isolation and spiritual pride; his to sociality and humbleness of mind. Theirs was a narrow brotherhood; his universal and complete. With the Essenes he could have little sympathy, certainly he drew from them no inspiration, and if he came into contact with them at all, it must have been in the way of opposition.

The sect of the Sadducees was more influential, in some respects the most influential of all, inasmuch as it embraced many members of the upper classes and of the higher ranks of the priesthood. Two of their leading tenets are known to us from the narrative of the Gospels. They said, we are told, that there is neither angel nor spirit, that there is no resurrection, no future punishment or reward ; and they recognised no other authority than that of the written law. These two positions have a close connection. Readers of the Old Testament Scriptures know how scanty are the references to a future state. Whatever the reason of the omission may be, of the fact there is no doubt, that among the numerous blessings and curses by which obedience to the law is recommended, and transgression of it restrained, no mention is made of those future rewards and punishments, the prospect of which seems to us so useful, if not necessary to influence human conduct. In the books of Moses especially, the subject is conspicuous by absence ; and our Lord in confuting the Sadducees from these books, adduces no direct statement of the truth, but finds it involved in the name of God.

This fact was recognised by both Pharisees and Sadducees. The former alleged it as a proof of the necessity of that supplement of oral or traditional revelation which they reverenced, and whose authority is upheld by most orthodox Jews down to the present day. The Sadducees on the other hand refused to acknowledge as authoritative anything but the written law. It does not appear that there is valid ground for the common opinion that they rejected all the ancient Scriptures except the Pentateuch ; but there is no doubt that they repudiated the traditions of the elders, whether in the shape of new revelations or of decisions and interpretations ; and it is probable that they regarded the later books of Scripture as possessed of an authority strictly subordinate to that of those which they believed to have been written by the lawgiver himself, and that nothing contained in the " Prophets " or " Writings " would for them establish a cardinal doctrine concerning which Moses had given no sign.

There could be no sympathy between Jesus and those haughty materialists, with their narrow conservatism as to the Word of God, and their Epicurean creed of " Let us eat and drink, for to-morrow we die." To them he was worse than the Pharisees, for he not only taught the immortality of the soul, and enforced the awful realities of a divine judgment, but seemed to slight and to supersede Moses himself. It is not strange that in presence of a teacher so searching, so humbling, so revolutionary, their enmity to their constant foes should have been held in check, and that they should have made common cause with them to compass his ruin.

The Pharisees occupy a much larger space in the Gospel narrative; and it is in conflict with them that the relation of Jesus to the religion of the time is most clearly defined. They sat in Moses' seat. By their direction the opinion and conduct of the masses were chiefly determined. Practically speaking, Judaism, by which term is here designated the religion of Israel in its decay, is the system of the Pharisees. "The righteousness of the Scribes and Pharisees" was the accepted model of piety.

The following are some of the leading characteristics of their method. It was purely formal and external. It recognised no heart-relation to God, no genuine spiritual life. It starved the emotional part of human nature, and left character to take care of itself. It treated man as a mere machine to be put through certain motions, and regarded heavenly blessings as prizes to be gained by rigid observance of certain outward forms. Do certain ceremonial acts; do not do certain other acts, in themselves good or indifferent, but pronounced to be unclean or dangerous by the tradition of the elders : and thus you will escape the damnation of hell, and secure the favour of God.

It was essentially a slavish righteousness. A purely mechanical obedience was to be rendered in a spirit of fear. It was like the forced labour of a slave under the lash of a taskmaster. Its object was to keep on the safe side of condemnation. God must be propitiated by sacrifices, satisfied with gifts, pleased and flattered by outward homage. The means of standing well with the Almighty being supposed to be accurately known and minutely described, every one who would escape his anger must use them with anxious and scrupulous care.

They laid stress on the negative rather than on the positive side of righteousness, and were chiefly concerned with the " Thou shalt nots " of the law. The Sabbath, for example, was nothing more to them than a restraint. God claimed for himself a certain portion of man's time, and would be offended if on that day anything were done by which ordinary profit or pleasure could be advanced. Keeping the Sabbath meant, not rejoicing in the divine boon of rest and using the opportunity of worship and mutual fellowship, but complying with every one of a multitude of puerile restrictions with which generations of purblind Scribes had hedged round the ancient commandment. The impotent man who carried his mat, the disciples who rubbed the ears of corn—it was with the muscular exertion and not the appropriation of the grain they found fault,—Jesus himself who opened the eyes of a blind man, were Sabbath-breakers in their view, and such actions amounted to deadliest sins.

Another feature of Pharisaic righteousness is, that as far as it had regard to moral conduct at all, it looked not on the spirit but on the letter of the law, and cared more for the outward behaviour than for the state of the heart. " So God was served in the letter," says Jeremy Taylor in one of his noblest sermons ; " they did not much inquire into his purpose ; and therefore they were curious to wash their hands, but cared not to purify their hearts ; they would give alms, but hate him that received it ; they would go to the temple, but did not revere the glory of God that dwelt there between the cherubims ; they would fast, but not mortify their lusts ; they would say good prayers, but not labour for the grace they prayed for. In moral duties where God expressed himself more plainly, they made no commentary of kindness, but regarded the prohibition so nakedly and divested of all antecedents, consequents, similitudes and properties, that if they stood clear of that hated name which was set down in Moses' tables, they gave themselves liberty, in many instances of the same kindred and alliance.   If they abstained from murder they thought it very well, though they made no scruple of murdering their brother's fame ; they would not cut his throat, but they would call him fool, or invent lies in secret, and publish his disgrace openly ; they would not dash out his brains, but they would be extremely and unreasonably angry with him ; they would not steal their brother's money, but they would oppress him in crafty and cruel bargains.   The commandment forbade them to commit adultery, but because fornication was not named, they made no scruple of that ; and being commanded to honour their father and mother, they would give them good words and fair observances, but because it was not named that they should maintain them in their need, they thought they did well enough to pretend 'corban,' and let their father starve."

Such were the Pharisees.   They were slaves of the letter, pedants in matters of form ; they would anxiously debate about the size of a frontlet, and wrangle over the breadth of a hem; they would settle to a yard the length of a Sabbath day's journey, and discuss with what sort of wick and oil candles might be lighted on that day; they would observe all the feasts commanded by Moses, or enjoined in the traditions, and repeat the appointed prayers the orthodox number of times; they would pay the due amount of tithes, and ostentatiously bestow the customary alms; and so would they build up their righteousness and serve the great God. All this they carried out with an astonishing pride, standing at the corners of the streets or in the temple to make their prayers, and thanking God that they were not as other men.

To such a pass had religion come among the children of Israel, the people who had Moses' law, and David's psalms, and Isaiah's visions of God. What need to say that to Jesus their doctrine embodied all that was falsest and most fatal in religious belief, and their lives all that was most detestable to a true and open soul?

While thus apart from all the sects, and especially hostile to the dominant form of religion, Jesus ever showed himself true to the genuine traditions of his people, to the spirit of Moses and Isaiah. But it was his mission to inaugurate a new epoch, to usher in a new dispensation ; and in doing so he must needs set aside much that was temporary and imperfect in the old. Himself observing the ancient ordinances, and to the last attending the national feasts, it was the inevitable result of his teaching that the old should pass away. When it was proclaimed that God is a spirit to be worshipped everywhere in spirit and in truth, the days of exclusive temple worship and national privilege were numbered. And it is no matter of wonder that zealous patriots should have regarded him with suspicion. For men are ever prone to confound form and substance, to give to the letter the reverence which is due to the spirit alone, and to elevate their creed, catechism, or other current interpretation of the writings to the level of the divine Word itself. To attack the Pharisees would be to many as if he had done dishonour to Moses, and to hold any but orthodox opinions about Moses and the books that go by his name was tantamount to blaspheming God. And there was more than this in the teaching of Jesus ; he did handle freely the ancient laws : he was not afraid to say that the law of divorce was imperfect, and to place his spiritual interpretation of leading commandments in opposition to that which was held by men of old time. He had come not to destroy but to fulfil, and his fulfilment seemed to many to involve dangerous tampering with revelation, and to be as bad as destruction. They could not see that he was carrying the old principles to their true issue, and stamping more deeply upon the human conscience the weightier matters of the law, the godly counsels of the prophets. And so he had to bear the reputation of an enemy of Israel and of God, and to die the death of a heretic and a blasphemer.

VIII.

THE KINGDOM OF HEAVEN.

Jesus found in the mouths of men two phrases which denoted the same thing, "kingdom of God" and "kingdom of heaven." John the Baptist had called upon men to repent because the kingdom was at hand, and the people crowded to his baptism. Jesus said, "the kingdom has come, repent and enter into it." At first the people rallied to the cry, but soon they forsook him and clamoured for his blood. He and they, as they discovered, using the same words—kingdom of God, Messiah, Son of God —meant by them very different ideas.

In the days of the exile there had slowly grown a hope that Jehovah would send a deliverer to restore the fallen fortunes of his people. The old stem of David would blossom in new beauty, and a servant of God would save Israel and bless all nations. The expectation took various forms. In the great prophecy which forms the concluding portion of the book of Isaiah, the Servant appears as a Man of Sorrows, in whom can almost be traced the very lineaments of the burdened Sufferer of Gethsemane and Calvary: but in other visions he is a royal warrior, revelling in conquest and vengeance, dyed in the blood of Israel's foes; and around this latter conception, after the spirit of prophecy had departed, the hopes of the oppressed nation chiefly gathered, so that the Messiah came to represent almost universally an actual descendant of David, who should expel the Romans from Jerusalem, and establish his throne in splendour and power. Psalms which, originally and historically, referred to David, Solomon, and Hezekiah, were read as literal descriptions of his glories; and darker pictures were dropped out of view.

So that, while in one sense it is true, as commonly stated, that Messianic expectations were a preparation for the coming of Christ, primarily they offered a chief hindrance to his reception. Before the people could receive him as alone he would be received, they must resign what to them was the substance of their Messianic hope; and this explains several places in the Gospel narrative which would otherwise be puzzling. For a Messiah after their own heart they longed with an enthusiasm to which both patriotism and piety lent their fires. Therefore they were not unwilling to believe in one who claimed the title, and under the charm of his discourse or the wonder of his miracles, were very ready to hail him as their king. To the last they hoped that he would throw off the character of Rabbi, which appeared a strange disguise, and present himself as David's glorious Son. They even tried to force him to adopt the bolder line. But when they found that instead of a call to arms he harped on the call to repentance—instead of proposals to set up his throne, treated them to sharp moral lectures, and bade them take up their cross and deny themselves, they left him, and at last were easily persuaded to turn against him in a fury of disappointed rage. What cared they for a Messiah who would not let his servants fight, and talked of a kingdom which was not of this world ?

Perhaps the popular conception of his kingdom now current, if not quite so gross and carnal, is not much more adequate than that of the multitude of Jerusalem. For we too fail to rise to the height of his grand simplicity and spirituality. When we read, " Blessed are the poor in spirit, for theirs is the kingdom of heaven," we do not think of an earthly kingdom to be set up speedily, whose honours and rewards are to be the portion of Christ's followers, but we may still think of something yet to come, and our hopes may be nearly as selfish and material as were those of the disciples. If " theirs is the kingdom of heaven," means to us only—they shall be saved, they shall not go to hell, they shall go to heaven, they shall enjoy the glories and pleasures which are the eternal inheritance of the redeemed,—we entertain an expectation by no means without foundation, which is full of comfort, which has been useful, and may yet be useful, to govern the conduct of men ; but we are not on the level of the thought of Jesus, and do not receive his words as spirit and life. His kingdom is a spiritual one, existing wherever there are humble, poor, and peaceable souls, seeking righteousness, loving God and the brethren. It is confined to no place and no time ; it is no rival of existing governments, but is above them all ; its laws are those of eternal love, its privileges peace and hope and holy joy. St. Paul understood his Master when he said that the " kingdom of

God is not meat and drink, but righteousness, and peace and joy in the Holy Ghost;" not meat and drink—no, nor rewards and privileges, and harps and crowns; not selfish advantages enjoyed now or hereafter, but deliverance from bondage, fear, and sin, victory over the world and death, fellowship with Christ in the Spirit, love to the brethren, and unbounded and un-questioning trust in the living God.

In calling men to enter the kingdom there is no doubt that he used very strong and peremp-tory language, as may be seen in his charge to the apostles when he sent them forth on an evangelistic mission. And it has seemed that he assumed somewhat too much, and that it was not strange that the people should not at once receive the message, or fair that those should be so severely blamed who failed so to do. But it must be understood that their error was not merely a political blunder. It would have been a hard case if, only because they misread the signs of the times, they should be so hardly judged as they are in several places of the New Testament. Neither was it merely a theological mistake. It would have been a hard case if they had been judged because they accepted the received interpretations, and fol-

lowed their accredited guides.   It was because
the question raised by the call of Jesus was a
moral and religious one that it was delivered
with so much authority, and that the doom of
those who would not listen was so severe ; for
when a message enters the religious sphere it
touches the conscience of responsible beings,
and raises the most solemn issues.   The gospel
had its political and its theological side, but it
was above all a message to the heart and conscience.   The call was plainly put as a call to
a change of life.   " Repent," was the burden of
John's preaching.   " Repent and believe," was
the call of Jesus.   On this point there was left
no room for doubt, and it was on this ground
that they who rejected the word of Jesus stood
condemned.

To modern minds the mention of the kingdom of God raises no vision of earthly grandeur,
no expectation of political change.   It has been,
perhaps, too thoroughly disengaged from earthly
politics.   But if we are thus in no danger of
being led astray by political conceptions, it is
otherwise with those that are theological.
What traditions of the elders and glosses of
the Scribes were to the Jews, are our systems
of theology and theories of redemption.   With

these the gospel of Jesus is too closely associated ; and when his call is addressed to men in its Calvinistic or other special form, they are apt to say, " It is a very hard case that we should be damned because we cannot receive a large number of tremendous and abstruse propositions in history, natural science, metaphysics, criticism, theology." A very hard case indeed this would be. But this must not hide from us the truth, which is, that Jesus deals with moral and spiritual ideas, and makes his appeal to the general conscience—claims general obedience to eternal principles of right. If a man is brought face to face with these fundamental things, as by the word of Jesus he unquestionably is, to that man " the kingdom of God has come nigh," and an issue has been raised which will not brook neglect or delay ; the choice of Hercules, the alternative of Joshua and Elijah, the narrow and the broad way of Jesus, have been set before him, and it is at his peril that he refuses to listen or chooses wrong.

IX.

THE SCRIPTURES.

THAT Jesus treated the ancient records of the religion of Israel with the utmost reverence needs not to be said. He by no means, however, uses them so slavishly as some would have us believe.

It is a favourite argument for the extreme orthodox view of the Bible that he attests the authority of Old Testament writers, and the authenticity of Old Testament history,— an argument useful when others more cognate to the matter have failed, and which the unfortunate critic is not permitted to call in question, on pain of being branded as an enemy of the faith. This is not a fair or sound argument. Without entering upon the burning questions concerning the composition and inspiration of the books of the Bible now agitating the church, a protest may be made against this altogether unwarranted and futile abuse of the great

Teacher's name. He used the Scriptures as he found them and as his hearers received them ; but on critical questions, which had not arisen, he gave no deliverance ; and it is unfair, alike to criticism and to him, to drag him in as an infallible authority. Besides, the fact is that when he has occasion to handle the Scriptures he does it, reverently indeed, but in a liberal and fearless fashion, as far as possible from the panic-stricken bibliolatry which now invokes his name, as the following examples show.

We read (Matt. xix. 3 ff.) that the Pharisees came unto him, tempting him, and saying unto him " Is it lawful for a man to put away his wife for every cause ?"   And he answered and said unto them, " Have ye not read that he which made them at the beginning made them male and female, and said, For this cause shall a man leave father and mother, and shall cleave to his wife : and they twain shall be one flesh ? Wherefore they are no more twain, but one flesh. What therefore God hath joined together let not man put asunder."

Upon this passage Dean Alford, whose authority, if not highest, is probably most extensive in this country, remarks—(1) " That our Lord refers to the Mosaic account of the creation as the historical fact of the creation of man, and grounds his argument on the literal expressions of the narrative. (2) That he cites both from the first and second chapters of Genesis, and in immediate connection, thus showing them to be consecutive parts of a continuous narrative, which, from their different diction, they have sometimes been supposed not to be. (3) That he quotes, as spoken by the Creator, the words in Gen. ii. 24, which were actually said by Adam ; they must therefore be understood as said in prophecy," etc. etc.

The truth is—(1) That our Lord refers to the fact that God made man male and female, and quotes from the narrative which was familiar to the Pharisees, and accepted by them as true : but this is no ground or excuse for alleging that he vouches for the Mosaic authorship of Genesis, or for the literal truth of the narrative of a creation in six days ; and it is something worse than absurd to persuade people who do not know any better, that the truth as it is in Jesus is bound up with the traditional view of these much disputed questions. (2) That he cites from the first and second chapters of Genesis, and in connection ; but readers can see for themselves that nothing is said or hinted

about the continuous connection of the chapters;
and no fair-minded person can fail to perceive
that our Lord's argument does not at all depend
on the composition of the book of Genesis,
but stands good although the first and second
chapters proceeded originally from different
hands, as by most educated people is now not
"supposed" but known, as surely as anything of
the kind can be known, to be the case.   (3)
That in all probability the words in question
are those of the author himself, and not of Adam;
and that, while they are properly enough cited
as expressing the mind of God on the subject,
the fact noticed by Alford really shows how
little Jesus, quoting as he did from memory,
cared for literal exactness of quotation.   If he
had the spirit of a passage, which he never failed
to seize and to exhibit clearly, he was not so
superstitiously anxious about the letter as the
Scribes of his and of our day.

The verses which follow are instructive in
another way.   "They say unto him, Why did
Moses then command to give her a writing of
divorcement, and to put her away?   He saith
unto them, Moses because of the hardness of
your hearts suffered you to put away your
wives : but from the beginning it was not so.

And I say unto you, Whosoever shall put away his wife, except it be for fornication, and shall marry another, committeth adultery : and whosoever marrieth her which is put away committeth adultery."

Here there is something more serious in question than the accuracy of ancient historical narratives, the soundness, namely, of moral principles, and the value of ancient precepts ; and far from vouching for the infallibility of the Scripture, he boldly declares its deliverance on a most important point of social morality to be imperfect and beneath the standard of primitive practice, an accommodation to the hard-heartedness of the race, a choice of a lesser evil,—and puts it aside in favour of a better law. We have the same principle applied in the Sermon on the Mount, but this is perhaps the most striking illustration of his attitude to the old covenant.

There is a very characteristic example in Luke ix. 51-56, to which it must suffice to refer very shortly. The inhabitants of a village in Samaria showed some discourtesy to Jesus and his company, because they were going up to the feast at Jerusalem. It was in that country, perhaps near the same place, that Elijah was said to have called down upon his enemies the vengeance of heavenly fire ; and the sons of Zebedee, with youthful zeal, burned to follow the old precedent : " but he turned and rebuked them, and said, Ye know not what manner of spirit ye are of. For the Son of man is not come to destroy men's lives, but to save." It may be too much to say, as has been said, that he rebukes Elias for what he had done in his day ; but he certainly rejects with some warmth the suggestion of following his example, and declares that the spirit of a deed, recorded without a sign of disapprobation in the Bible, was utterly alien from his own.

This deserves to be pondered by those who are perplexed by the moral difficulties of the Old Testament, and think themselves bound to account as good what their heart and conscience rise against as evil. Jesus does not require us to approve of even a judicial severity like that of Elijah, and still less of such things as the extermination of the Canaanites, and the atrocities of the conquest, and the murder of Eglon or of Sisera, or to admire and adopt the curses of the 109th Psalm. Such things might be done and said by them of old time, but he hath shown us a better way. To make him responsible for them all, as ultra-conservative criticism—in this, as in many things, so terribly destructive—is foolish enough to do, is wholly without excuse. When writers of that school urge that a minatory psalm is the utterance of the Spirit of God with reference to Judas, or that Christ himself must be principally understood as the person speaking, they must be answered in plain words. It is not to be endured that men, even with good intent, should so blaspheme his blessed name. The Christ of the Gospels the speaker in the 109th Psalm! Have they who venture to say so ever read these words, " Love your enemies, bless them that curse you ; and pray for them that despitefully use you and persecute you"? And do they know that, himself following his own high rule, he is credibly reported with his dying breath to have said, " Father, forgive them, for they know not what they do "?

X.

THE FATHER.

THEY who want proofs of the being of God must seek for them elsewhere than in the Gospels. Newton nowhere proves the existence of the sun, and in none of his recorded discourses does Jesus offer any argument about the existence of God. Readers may smile, and say, We see the sun, but God we cannot see. True : but there is an eye of the spirit, which some men trust as implicitly as the eye of the body ; and no one can read the words of Jesus without perceiving that the love of God is as certain to him as the light of the sun. We may believe that he could have supported his position by argument if he had chosen ; but apparently he did not choose. It would probably have, to his own mind, seemed superfluous and absurd; besides, it was not called for by any antagonistic opinion, speculative atheism being a form of error which in all probability never came in his way.

Further, those who cannot dispense with precise logical definitions of the nature of the Godhead, need not look for them here. These are a product of Western ingenuity ; they would not have been useful to Christ's hearers ; perhaps they might not have been altogether satisfactory to him. At all events they are out of his province, which is not logic but religion ; not formal exposition but spiritual revelation. "No man hath seen God at any time :" no man hath proved God if mathematical demonstration be required ; "the only begotten Son hath declared him." In respect of this fundamental article, as of others in religion, we walk by faith, not by sight.

Himself fully conscious, not only that God is, but that he is in close fellowship with him, speaking to people whose consciousness of God had been moulded by the Scriptures and by the peculiar history of their race—to men who might have very imperfect, and even false, notions concerning God, but who, like himself, had mostly no more doubt as to his existence than they felt concerning their own—Jesus says : "After this manner pray ye, Our Father

which art in heaven;" and teaches that the
secret of true prayer is in the confidence that
"your Father knoweth what things ye have
need of, before ye ask him."   The motive and
the goal of spiritual progress is that "ye may
be perfect, even as your Father in heaven is
perfect."   The word of Jesus is his Father's
word; his work, the work the Father had
given him to do; his life was doing the Father's
will; his death going to the Father's house.
This conviction of divine Fatherhood is the
foundation of all his teaching; it pervades his
words—the Sermon on the Mount no less than
the intercessory prayer recorded in the Gospel
according to St. John; it is the key to his
theology, the ground of his ethics, the secret of
his comfort.   The end of his mission is to give
to as many as receive him "power to become
sons of God."

Which we are told was all very well in that
simple early time, but is quite unsuited to our
more advanced ideas. 'It is pure anthropomorphism.' Perhaps it is. There are two kinds of
anthropomorphism—the one resting on the idea
that the gods must be made in the image of
man, the other on the ancient truth that God
made man in his own image. If men think

that God is altogether such an one as themselves, and attribute to their deities—for this is
generally found in connection with polytheism
—their parts, passions, weaknesses, and people
heaven with a crowd of non-natural men of
larger stature, greater strength, and fouler lusts ;
if thus man makes gods in his own image, the
result is certainly not to be admired. But if,
on the other hand, it is true that God made
man in his own likeness, and that there is a real
kindred between him and the spirit that is in
man ; then, so far from its being unreasonable to
find in what is best in human nature a revelation of the divine, and in earthly relationships a
shadow of heavenly things, it is hard to see how
divine truth can be otherwise communicated, or
how, except in such human forms, we can think
of God at all. Philosophers may say that it is
absurd to attribute personality to the absolute
and infinite, but none the less is it certain that
religious persons will continue to regard God as
a living being, manifesting himself to them
under the form of personality; and this belief of
theirs, though it neither is, nor pretends to be,
in the order of philosophical ideas, may be perfectly consistent with those of them that are
true. The doctrine of Jesus is, to many minds

—they may be unphilosophical, but they are sound, and not untrained in philosophical thinking,—every way more satisfactory than any which philosophy has offered in its place. Of these the most familiar to the English public is the definition offered by Mr. Arnold, who, insisting on allowing no conception which cannot be scientifically verified, finds, as the residuum of his analysis, these two things :—" A stream of tendency in all things to fulfil the law of their being," and " an eternal power, not ourselves, which makes for righteousness." We must be pardoned if we think this new formula fully as crabbed and quite as difficult of verification as some of those ancient ones Mr. Arnold criticises with such irrepressible scorn ; but we may let that pass. The wonderful thing is that this should be announced to-day as the outcome of the best modern light. To say nothing of the doctrine of St. Paul, the Stoic philosophers whom he met at Athens could have told him something as good as this, if not better. And for this we, and especially the simple-hearted but hard-headed workmen among us, are asked to give up our faith in the Father of Jesus ! It is not probable that we shall, and it does not appear very evident why we should. These definitions are by no means hard to accept, and supposing them to be absolutely correct, they are not inconsistent with the Christian belief; for this stream of tendency may have been impressed on things by the Father of our spirits, and the evidences of this mysterious power making for righteousness may be the expression of his will. Again be it said, there are minds to which this hypothesis seems not only rational but the only one which rationally accounts for what we see; and there are hearts, millions of them, to whom it supplies a sure foundation for their faith and hope in the realm of the unseen.

God is the Father of spirits, whom men may love, and to whom men are very dear. By the love he has planted in their own bosoms Jesus teaches them to know what is in the heart of God; and in his own life he offers a true image of the glory of divine righteousness. If it be anthropomorphism to believe that God is the Father of Jesus, to that we willingly plead guilty; for in this faith do we live, and in it we desire to grow more and more.

It is an essential part of our belief that God is perfect. This is the message his disciples always heard of Jesus, and declare to the world, that "God is light, and in him is no darkness at all." How we need this message now! How have men turned the light into darkness that is sorely felt! How many of us take our ideas of God not from Christ, but from imperfect human systems, and from misconceptions of these—childish caricatures of a true theology! If this were not apparent from the language of believers, it would be abundantly shown by the infidelity which floats on the surface of shallow minds, or froths into flippant speech; and it is very evident from the style of late assaults upon Christianity. Not to mention living names, no one who understands such a poet as Shelley can fail to see that he must have strangely and even ludicrously misapprehended the faith he attacks with such wildness of hate. Whether the fault of this lay most with him or with those from whom he derived his ideas of Christian truth, who in his day sat in Christ's seat and spoke in his name, may for the present be left undetermined; but there is no doubt that the God he blasphemes is not our God,—not the God of the New Testament, but the God of the church grossly misconceived. Were he such an one as Shelley fancied, he was not wrong to refuse to love and worship him; he did right to renounce and defy him. No pious soul should ever be persuaded to believe that there is any darkness in "the Eternal." We should be cautious and humble, not too ready to transfer to our thought of God what may be only stains on our own conscience, or to take the motes of our imagination for spots on the Sun of righteousness; but we should steadfastly refuse to believe that there is anything evil in our Father that is in heaven, anything which we should call wrong if we heard it said of a father upon earth, anything but what is highest, purest, brightest, and best; we should rather doubt the authority of the church, the interpretation of the Bible, the power of our own understanding—we should doubt everything rather than the truth of the message learned from Jesus, that "God is Light, and in him is no darkness at all."

XI.

SONSHIP.

In this idea of divine Fatherhood that of human sonship is involved. God a perfect Father, man his erring child ; these are complementary truths, and they are so treated by our Lord. But we have somehow got into sad confusion on the subject of our relation to God, and it is difficult now-a-days to speak to men as Jesus did, without being suspected of dangerous heresy. With our theories of baptism, and our doctrines of conversion, and our distinctions between general and Christian sonship, our ideas on this important point are in general far from clear.

Keeping to the words of Jesus, we find that he speaks of their Father in heaven to all sorts and conditions of men, appeals to this relation as the largest and deepest fact of their being, and seeks on the consciousness of it to build up a new life. He also speaks of divine sonship as a thing to be striven for. "Your reward shall be great, and ye shall be the children of your Father in heaven ;" (do such and such things) "that ye may be the children of your Father." And John says that "to as many as received him" he gave "power to become sons of God."

In presence of these facts it is impossible to maintain a very common opinion that it is only of believers—of those who have received the power of which John speaks that God is the Father. Nor is there any real foundation for the distinction so commonly assumed between general and special Fatherhood, which is a pure invention to meet the supposed exigencies of the theological problem. The two positions are reconciled when we do what it is the first step in sound religious thinking to learn to do,—when we remember that there is in truth an infinite and a finite element, a divine ideal and a human fact, a side turned towards God and a side turned towards man.

The truth on the divine side is that which we have considered in the foregoing chapter. God is the Father of men. That is an eternal fact. It is not created by our faith, it does not depend on anything in us whatsoever ; neither does our unbelief make it of none effect. Paul was not afraid to quote in the hearing of many Athenians, who will hardly be claimed as being of the number of the elect, the verse of the heathen poet, " we are also his offspring."

When, however, we turn to the other side, we pass from a region where we can make absolute and universal statements to one where everything is broken and imperfect. Mankind do not fulfil the ideal of sonship. They require to be instructed concerning their birthright, brought back to the father, reconciled to him, trained in filial duty and obedience ; and therefore, as matter of fact, they are not children of God, do not feel themselves so to be, and need to have power given them so to " become." When St. Paul desires to express the whole truth in one sentence, he has to say, " Ye are all the children of God by faith in Christ Jesus ;" not that faith, as some vainly think, makes God our Father, but that it enables us to know that he is, and to receive the spirit of sons.

Perhaps this is too formal ; here is another view of the matter. When in familiar speech we say of a man that he is his father's son, we use words which, interpreted strictly and literally, convey no meaning, inasmuch as every man must be the son of his father ; but we are understood to signify that, in regard to some observed qualities, to outward appearance and gait, to habit or character, he is like his father, so like that any one who knows the father must recognise him as his son. Thus we interpret more than one saying of our Lord's in which he virtually exhorts us to be our Father's children, to be like him, so that men may know us for his children, and own that we are not unworthy of such a name.

In the stories of childhood, and the poetry to which we turn as we grow older, we have read of a king's son being brought up in a peasant's cottage, living from year to year in ignorance of his rank, playing with the peasant's children, sharing their humble fare, and bearing the burden of their rustic toil. A youth, placed in such circumstances, is, and is not, a king's son. He is, because so he was born, and his blood and race cannot be changed ; he is not, because he knows it not, and the feelings and habits proper to his birth have not been developed. When, however, the messengers come from the Court to hail him as their prince, and clothe him with royal apparel, there dawns upon him the con- sciousness of his real destiny, and he begins to feel that he is a king's son. But more than this is needed before he can be so in reality; he must be taught to lay aside the rustic language and habits of his childhood, to assume the bearing and manners of his rank, to learn its duties, and meet its responsibilities, and so to be in fact as he is by right, the son of a king. "Beloved," says St. John, " now are we the sons of God; and it doth not yet appear what we shall be, but we know that when he shall appear we shall be like him, for we shall see him as he is. And every man that hath this hope in him purifieth himself, even as he is pure."

We ought perhaps to have been content with our Lord's own illustration, which is the best. The youth whom we call the prodigal was, all through his career, his father's son. We can trace, however, various stages of experience through which he passed. When he began to grow weary of the quiet and orderly life of home, to lose delight in his father's society, and despise the work his father gave him to do, the spiritual bond between them was strained; when he demanded his portion and went away, it was on the son's side snapped in twain, as the father recognised, when, without a word of remonstrance, he let him go. In the far country, wasting his substance with riotous living, he was not his father's son; he had lost all sympathy with his father, had quenched love, had renounced obedience, had dishonoured the name, and had therefore, concerning all that makes the reality of sonship, become, as his father said, dead. When he came to himself, and confessed that he was no longer worthy to be called a son, the filial feeling began to revive; it taught him that if anywhere in all the world there was hope for him it was in the love of the father he had wronged; it urged him to arise, and go and confess, and beg for mercy; it grew in him as he journeyed homewards; and it was perfectly restored when he lay in his father's arms, and felt his father's kiss, and when, with the ring on his finger, and the robe of honour around him, he sat in his father's house a son once more. "This my son was dead and is alive again, and was lost and is found." The veil of allegory in that beautiful parable is very thin, and beyond all doubt we have here the truth of this subject "as it is in Jesus."

Very much deeper truth, it must be observed, than that which is contained in the theological doctrine of adoption. As a question of logic it is difficult to see how that doctrine deserves to be separated from that of justification, from which it scarcely differs, except in form and expression ; but with that question we are not concerned.   It does, however, concern us to point out, especially to those who have been instructed in the Catechism of the Westminster divines, that there is a great deal more in the doctrine of Jesus than this, that believers " are received into the number, and have a right to all the privileges of the sons of God."   It is curious to note that to these words is appended, as a proof text, the verse already quoted from St. John : " As many as received him, to them gave he power to become the sons of God, even to them that believe on his name ;" as if they had adequately expressed the truth of that statement, and exhausted its blessedness ; as if they had not plainly omitted its chief element, without which the rest would be a very small thing indeed.   We want more than enrolment in the number, and investment with privileges, before we can be called sons of God.   We want to have the feelings proper to sons, to be made partakers of the divine nature, to be sons in deed and in truth ; and this we get through Christ.   Any man, by a stroke of his pen, may adopt a boy, take him into his family, confer upon him all the rights and privileges he would have inherited had he been by birth his own child ; but he cannot so easily secure his affection, or make him such as he would like a son of his to be. Even so might a child of the devil be taken into the household of God, and endowed with all the privileges of the children, and, so far from being made a true son, be tenfold more the child of sin than he was before. In the Westminster Confession an addition is made to the above quoted definition of adoption, which might with advantage have been embodied in the manual for the young : " Have his name put upon them ; receive the spirit of adoption ; have access to the throne of grace with boldness ; are enabled to cry, Abba, Father ; are pitied, protected, provided for, and chastened by him as a Father." It is the spirit of adoption that is the great thing, and this spirit—whereby a man can call God his Father, and love him with all his heart, and delight in the doing of his will—it is the work of Jesus to bestow.

XII.

LOVE TO GOD.

LOVE is the essence of sonship, and therefore love is the fulfilling of the law. This is the first and great commandment: "Thou shalt love the Lord thy God with all thy heart, and with all thy soul, and with all thy strength, and with all thy mind."

Thou shalt love! Can any creature then, it is asked, love at the word of command? "Can men in general take up the words of the Psalmist and say: 'I will love thee, O Lord, my strength'? I may resolve to obey him, to worship him, but I cannot answer for my love. His perfection awes me, and makes my heart chill for fear; and with full conviction that God is worthy to be loved, with every desire to live in so delightful relation towards him, I may not be able to obey this first and great commandment." This is a conceivable course of thought, and perhaps represents the experience, partial and fleeting indeed, but none the less genuine experience of honest persons who have searched their hearts and tried to keep this law.

There is something like a paradox in making love a matter of duty. Love is nothing if not spontaneous, hearty, and unconstrained. Still we may reflect that in regard to natural affections we acknowledge a distinct obligation, and though they are not directly under the control of the will, give diligence for their regulation. Nature bids a man love his father and mother, and society visits with condemnation any one who transgresses this first commandment of natural law. So does religion enjoin the love of our Father in heaven.

Moreover, there are certain qualities and certain services, the presence of which qualities and the rendering of which services are recognised as claiming love and gratitude. If there be in a community a man of noble and winning character, beloved by all wise and good men, who has shown us signal kindness, we should hardly venture to say to any person whose good opinion we value that we did not love him ; and we should certainly expect that if we loudly declared that love will not come unbidden, and that we could not render it in this case, we should be told that we were pronouncing our own condemnation, or at least proclaiming a defect which might well cause us serious concern, if not shame.   So it is not extravagant for true religion, which reveals the adorable perfection and supreme beneficence of the Most High, to declare that in the knowledge of him consisteth life eternal, and in the love of him lieth the whole duty of man.

' Yes, but suppose I admit this fully, but confess, with sorrow and shame if you like, that I cannot honestly say that I feel towards God this supreme affection, and that I do not see how I am to cure my defect, if defect it be, what has religion to say ? '

This first, that when a man really wishes to love God, and regrets the absence of love, he is not far from the kingdom of heaven.   " If with all your heart ye truly seek me, ye shall surely find me."   God is nearer to such persons than they suppose, and their wisdom lies not in sighing for an ideal perfection, but in cherishing the grace they have received, in seeking to advance in the knowledge of God, and above all, in faithfully endeavouring to do his will. There are men amongst us at present, not a few, that make little religious profession, and are very much at sea concerning religious belief, who love goodness with an almost passionate ardour, whose hearts swell when they hear of a generous action, and who rejoice in the triumph of a good cause and the success of good men. Theirs is certainly not such love to God as Jesus felt and wishes us to feel, but it is love to him nevertheless, for all this is of him ; and it were good for them and for the world if they could learn to concentrate their vague sentiment in living affection upon the Almighty and All-merciful Father of all.

This next we have to say to those who desire to love God, but cannot find it in their hearts so to do : that there are obstacles which may hinder us, and which we must endeavour to remove.

Of which the first and most obvious is, that " men love darkness rather than light, because their deeds are evil." " If the world hate you," said Jesus to his disciples, " ye know that it hated me before it hated you. He that hateth me hateth my Father also." On this point it is unnecessary in this place to dwell.

Many are hindered by selfishness and a worldly habit. We may be pure in our living, sober, honest, neighbourly, and thoroughly respectable, and yet have no love to God. "If any man love the world, the love of the Father is not in him." This does not mean that we cannot love God if we admire this beautiful earth in which we live, if we are keenly interested in contemporary history, if we heartily enjoy the company of our fellow-creatures, if we are fond of music and painting, and laughter and games, and find the world, with all its toils and cares, its wars and crimes, a kindly and pleasant place upon the whole. All that, instead of hindering, should help us to love God ; and true religion, far from discouraging it, is ready to encourage us to love the world in that way better and more wisely than we mostly do. But if we love the world in a low and selfish fashion, with an animal affection, or a cold aesthetic admiration ; if we love it exclusively or excessively; then the love of the world becomes a snare, and a serious hindrance to our obedience to the first and great commandment of the spiritual life.

Others are hindered by the difficulty they find in realising the presence of him who is invisible. Partly from dulness of imagination, partly it may be, from that slowness of heart of which Jesus complains so much, there are many who do not feel that God is one with whom they have to do. They are not atheists, and may even be horrified to think that such persons are suffered to live ; they are orthodox, and like discussions about God's attributes and decrees ; but he is not to them, as he was to the singers of Israel, a sun and shield, a refuge and de-liverer, a shepherd and ever present friend ; not as to Jesus, a Father who has loved them always, and never leaves them alone. A great want, even among people supposed to have had a good religious education, and whose religious character is above suspicion, is to be brought to believe that there is a living God ; and closely connected with this is the cognate need of understanding that they are themselves living souls.

Others still are kept from the love of God by mistaken views or theories concerning him. A man sits down and broods and meditates, and out of his own false notions, or diseased fancies, makes a monster, which he calls God, and then quite honestly and most naturally says: 'I cannot love this being, I stand in awe of him, I fear him, but love him I cannot, for he is anything but an amiable being.' Or he takes his ideas of God from others—it may be from the dead words of fanatics dead long ago ; he hears God's plan of salvation, as it is called, described so as to represent him as unjust, capricious, hard, and stern, and he cries out bitterly like the poet mentioned on a former page, " I cannot love the God of whom these men speak, I hate him with all my heart and soul."   There is no doubt that bad theology is the cause of a great deal of the alienation from religion which at present exists ; and that we need to go back and learn from Jesus to know the true God, and to look up with him and say, " Our Father which art in heaven."

Some sincere souls are doubtless kept from loving God by their thoughts concerning the darker aspects of his providence.   Clouds and darkness are round about him, and his ways seem often to be relentless and cruel.   As men count wealth and evil, it is often ill with the righteous and well with the wicked ; and even with larger and purer views of welfare, it is often hard to believe in the righteousness of his rule. And men looking too much on such dark things, grow sad and bitter, and murmur or rail against him and say : ' What ! love one who can sit still and witness, or, as you teach, direct such hideous catastrophes, who heeds not the cry of

the oppressed, and will not restrain the violence
of men!' Jesus who heard of the Galileans
slaughtered by Pilate, and the eighteen crushed
by the tower of Siloam, and declared that these
things did not happen to them on account of
their sins, who prayed for deliverance from his
own fate, and cried out on the cross, " My God,
my God, why hast thou forsaken me?" could
still trust in God, and commit his spirit unto
him ; and bids us not let our hearts be troubled,
but trust and leave secret things to him.   And
we may be helped to this if we think that he
knows all these things far better than we, sees
further into them, feels them more keenly, and
is making them all work together for good.
After all, though the dark spots are dark, and
far from small, the light in most lives is im-
mensely larger, and is very bright if we were
not somewhat carelessly blind ; and though
there are things which are hard to be understood, they are not to be compared to the
glory of his kindness which is revealed.   There
are days in the year gloomy and full of
storm and wreck, and on the brightest, clouds
may obscure the blessed sun ; but there are
bright days too, and on the darkest the sun is
still shining behind the cloud ; other eyes, if not
ours, see his glory, and we too, if we have

patience, shall yet rejoice in the brightness of his shining and the warmth of his rays.

Our second answer to our friend who wanted to love God but could not, has grown to unexpected length. It was to the effect that he should consider what obstacles may hinder him, and examples of these presented themselves which led us on, it must be hoped not unprofitably.

There is yet another answer which religion has to offer to such appeals, which shall not detain us so long, but may not on any account be omitted. It is that we must draw near to God, and in this, as in all things, cast ourselves on his help. No part of Jesus' teaching is to be received without that which was the dear and constant habit of his spirit, and has been the cherished resort of his best and happiest scholars—prayer. If we would keep the first and great commandment, let us say " God be merciful unto us, and bless us, and incline our hearts to keep this law."

" O Lord, who hast prepared for them that love thee such good things as pass man's understanding, pour into our hearts such love towards thee, that we, loving thee above all things, may obtain thy promises, which exceed all that we can desire."

XIII.

LOVE TO MAN.

"AND the second is like unto it, namely;
Thou shalt love thy neighbour as thyself."

God is supremely worthy to be loved, and
we can be told that if we do not render him
the affection which is due, this argues something seriously wrong with ourselves. Is it so
with man? is he so amiable in himself that he
needs only to be truly known in order to be
wholly loved? and if not, is it reasonable to say,
"thou shalt love thy neighbour?" It is all very
well to say fine things about brotherhood and
the law of love; but when an honest man
takes it to himself, and applies it to individual
specimens of the human race—says to himself,
'My master bids me love every human creature,
the worst and vilest, bids me love such an one
who has maligned me, such another who has for
his own pleasure dragged a woman trusting him
too fondly into ruin of body and soul,' he

recognises the exceeding breadth of the commandment, and the greatness of Christian righteousness ; he is even tempted to say, ' Lord, I cannot do this ; I may be kind to poor people, I may forgive my enemy, I will try to pass a seducer or a hypocrite without striking him or cursing him, but I am afraid I cannot pretend, and need not try, to love every man who is my neighbour; I can only love that which is pleasant to my heart and is worthy to be loved.' What, on the part of religion, have we to say to this ?

We might say that the law is, " Love thy neighbour as thyself," and that no man is so immaculate himself as to have a right to bear hardly on his neighbour : that this is Christ's commandment, " That ye love one another, as I have loved you." But we shall begin by pointing out the danger of confusion of terms.

We have no other word wherewith to describe this grace than that which we apply to our partial human affections, and which is conventionally assigned in an especial manner to that which is the most exclusive, and often the most selfish of them all. Our translators have in the thirteenth chapter of the first Epistle to the Corinthians, employed the word charity ;

but that is still more decidedly associated with restricted meanings. Benevolence is too cold ; philanthropy too hard. One of the latest and freshest writers on the subject, has chosen the phrase, "enthusiasm of humanity." We retain the old word love ; but we must bear in mind that Jesus is at pains to warn us that it means something greater and wider than natural affection or personal inclination. It is of the very nature of such affection that it distinguishes and selects ; it is the glory of Christian love that, aiming to be like that of the Father, it embraces all.

We have next to point out that the love of our brother does not imply admiration of his character or approval of his conduct ; does not, in fact, depend on what would be called his amiability at all. We are to love him because he is our brother. Even in earthly attachments we have experience of affection which is bestowed in spite of the presence of unattractive qualities, and defies unworthiness and outrage. It is so in natural relationships, where we not only expect mothers to love their children independently of their personal claims, but are not surprised to see them lavish their tenderest affection on the weakest and worst member of their families. It is so even in our personal likings and friendships ; we can continue to like men whom we cannot always admire, and like them perhaps better than better men.

We may profitably reflect also that we believe that God, the pure and perfect one, who cannot look upon iniquity, loves us all, imperfect and sinful though we be. Is it for our beauty or holiness—because we are, as we say, amiable creatures in his sight ? If he can love us, is there any fellow-creature so far beneath our regards as we might seem to be beneath those of the Highest ? If he loves the poorest, meanest, wickedest of his children, are we to call any of our brethren whom he loveth common or unclean ?

This indeed is what we must learn, to think that our neighbour is a child of God, a brother in Christ ; to realise the fatherhood of God and the brotherhood of men, not as fine phrases and figures of speech, but as spiritual facts, the deepest and firmest we know ; to believe that the new commandment in which Jesus takes up the old that was from the beginning, rests on a real relationship, not narrow like those of earth, but wide as the heavens. The noble line of the Roman poet, in which he calls himself man, and declares that he counts nothing human foreign to himself, expresses a sentiment which becomes a living truth to one who, through Jesus, has come to see in all that is human something that is divine.

'Something that is divine. Are we not getting out of the rational line we have affected, and, wandering into that of hazy and dogmatic assumption? Is not this a little too strong?' Not if it is true that God made man in his image, and that it was possible for Jesus to call himself Son of man and Son of God. No matter though the image be hidden and defiled, though it require to be unveiled and restored; if it is there, if man as man has certain faculties which separate him from the apes, to whom, on the physical side, he is so closely allied; if he has been made only a little lower than angels, and has capacities of divine endeavour, and possibilities of endless improvement; if, in short, the word of Jesus is true that he is a child of the Highest, then it is sober truth that in the earthen vessel of humanity lies a treasure which is divine. And even as we are wont to say of an uncouth rustic that he has in him the making of a good ploughman or a smart soldier, or of an uneducated boy that he has the qualities which, if cultivated, would make him shine as a lawyer or as a poet ; as in either case we should delight to watch and to further the development of latent energies, and to open to them a worthy career ; so, does Jesus teach us to see in every man the making of a Christian, to believe that it is the birthright of all men to be good and pure, to trust that it is the purpose of God to bring them to glory, honour, immortality, eternal life.

This is what St. Paul means when he speaks of Christ being in all, and teaches that in presence of this common element and bond of union all lesser distinctions disappear. It is good to get down to fundamental relations and to bring the larger sympathies into play. We have divisions enough in this country. We have our distinctions of rank, and class and profession, and creed and party. Employers and employed, Tories and Radicals, churchmen and disestablishers, fill the air with the noise of their contendings. But let danger seriously threaten the old country, and we should see party and even sectarian strife hushed, and class jealousies forgotten, and private feuds dropped, as men of all ranks and conditions stood shoulder to shoulder, filled with the genial glow of a common patriotism.   It is the purpose of Jesus to call to life a yet deeper love, and appeal to a broader sympathy, when he teaches men, not now and then, but always, to remember that they are all members of the kingdom of heaven, " fellow-citizens of the saints and of the household of God."   In the power of this truth we know how unnatural are those passions of wrath, envy, malice, which, speaking of human nature as it is, we call natural ; how alien they are to our true nature as children of God ; how truly natural and reasonable it is that we should love one another ; how simple it seems that we should deny ourselves, and seek every man the good of others, and even, should it be so required, lay down our lives for the brethren.   Perhaps we shall thus understand how it is that there are some who think that the selfish Christianity which has been so much in vogue — the egotism of converts caring for nothing but the safety of their own souls—is a poor representative of the religion of Jesus ; and that there is a great work and a great career open to any church which, leaving the barren wastes of dogma, and the uncertain and often morbid atmosphere of excited feeling, should set itself to hold up with proper faithfulness, and work out with proper persistency, the idea of a genuinely brotherly life,—should endeavour more adequately to teach and fulfil that which is acknowledged to be, by way of excellence, the law of Christ.

Lastly, let none suppose that because this law is reasonable it is easy of fulfilment. It is a counsel of perfection, which, being beyond mere human power, needs more than human help. This Jesus does not conceal, but rather is anxious to show. Of this, as of all his precepts, it is avowed that they are not mere ethical maxims, but religious laws, based on religious truth, supported by religious considerations, and to be received and obeyed in a religious spirit. Of the law of love this is especially and expressly said. In the fifteenth chapter of John's Gospel, in the parable of the vine, which, whatever its history and value may be from a critical point of view, is substantially authentic and undoubtedly true, we read thus: "Abide in me, and I in you. As the branch cannot bear fruit of itself, except it abide in the vine, no more can ye, except ye abide in me. These things I command you, that ye love one another." He commands us; it is our duty; but we shall never do it except we abide in him.

XIV.

THE GOLDEN RULE.

THE law of Christ, turned into a handy rule for working, is this: "All things whatsoever ye would that men should do unto you, do ye even so unto them." It is idle to dispute whether or not this is an original precept. The claim of Jesus to our regard rests not upon sole possession of truth, or original invention of statements ; but rather on his teaching us to see, and enabling us to act upon, universal and eternal truth. It is, however, a significant fact that this rule, at least in the Rabbinical versions of it, appears in the negative form ; and it is not particularly creditable to modern Christianity that it so seldom gets beyond the old reading : "Don't do to others what ye would not like them to do to you." That, doubtless, is necessary, and much would be gained for the world if even in that form the rule were followed, if we never did things to others which we should object to have done to us, or said things about our neighbours which we should be angry or sorry to have said about us; but though we should attain to that, we should not fulfil the law of Christ, which is positive, absolute, and exceeding broad,—" Do to others as you would have others do to you."

It is a very handy rule. In the greater number of cases, at least in private life, we shall easily see what we ought to do if we put ourselves in our brother's place, and think what we should like him to do to us if our relative positions were changed. It being presupposed that the laws of justice are always observed, and that we consult the real welfare of ourselves and others, this will generally be a sufficient guide. If circumstances arise, as they may, in which difficulty presents itself, we must exercise our best judgment; if we wish to go into the casuistry of the subject, and consider how the rule is to be applied in the various relations of a complicated social system, we shall not want counsellors; but if we love our neighbours as ourselves, and really want to do them good, we shall not go far astray as long as we follow this rule. We may make mistakes; but we shall never do a great wrong.

It would be grossly extravagant to represent society as systematically neglecting this, and acting upon motives of a purely selfish kind. Selfishness and hatred are disruptive forces, and if they were supreme society could not hold together for a day. If it is our happiness to belong to a community in which some order and good fellowship are to be found, we may be sure that, directly or indirectly, the law must to a considerable extent be obeyed. Nay, we know it is. I, at all events, have met with much more of kindness than of injury and ill-will in the course of my life ; and in my goings out and in among my neighbours have seen enough of neighbourliness and self-sacrifice to make me lean more to the optimist than to the pessimist view of human nature.

But for all that, there is much need of a more constant and earnest endeavour in this direction. Especially is there room for improvement in social and political affairs. Not individuals only, but classes of men, must learn to look not on their own things but also on the things of others. The hard and often cruel operation of economical laws must be tempered by the spirit of pity and brotherly kindness ; and until this is learned, neither by strikes nor lockings-out, nor by arbitrations and co-operations, can the disorders of our social and industrial system be remedied. Things are mending in this respect ; we are coming more to realise that we are members one of another, and to acknowledge obligations beyond the sphere of kindred and friendship ; corporations and societies are required to have something like a conscience, and even to show mercy occasionally ; and it is becoming evident to many who have no love for current forms of Christianity, that it is only on the lines laid down by Christ that the various problems which arise out of the mutual relation of classes and parties are to be solved.

In the sphere of high politics it does not now sound so absurd as once it would have done, even to Christian statesmen, to put forward the golden rule as the fundamental article of the International Code. There are in this country leading politicians who allow this, and there are even some of the first rank who try to act upon this principle, who are not ashamed to hold that nations as well as private men are bound to love and not to hate one another, and that their wisest and noblest course is to be honest, generous, and forbearing. The best account yet given of the causes of war is that offered by St. James — wars and fightings come of the lusts which war in our members. While the lusts remain so will the wars ; when they are cast out, and love takes their place, then, and not sooner, may be fulfilled the vision which a prophet saw long ago, and which still we can only behold afar off, when nation shall not rise up against nation, and they shall not study war any more.

The reason annexed to this commandment deserves more attention than it commonly receives.   The first word of this often quoted verse is "therefore ;" and looking back, we see that it means because your heavenly Father giveth good things to all, because ye are the children of God and must be like him in his pure and unstinted goodness.   We note this, not only because it shows us in what spirit and under what motive the law is to be obeyed, —like the "abide in me," quoted in the end of last section ; but because it marks the difference between a purely utilitarian or prudent maxim and a Christian precept, between philosophical ethics and religion.   Jesus is distinctively a religious teacher ; eminently rational in the best sense of the term, but the reverse of rationalistic. The religious element is everywhere prominent ; in the synoptic as much as in the Johannine version of his doctrine ; in the Sermon on the Mount, as strongly as in the talk with Nicodemus or the last great supplication. The contrary of this is often assumed in present discussions, but the position cannot be maintained. That the Lord's words, as reported by John, bear strongly the impress of the writer's brooding habit and peculiar style, no careful reader can fail to see ; but that in them alone is a divine element to be found, candid readers will hardly be persuaded to believe. To contrast the " simple and rational morality," of the discourses recorded by Matthew with the " mystical theology " of those contained in the Gospel according to St. John, is even more unjust to the synoptical than it is to the Johannine version. It is surprising to find any one who has really studied the Sermon on the Mount, speak of it as a piece of mere ethical teaching, which represents the real doctrine of Jesus, as contrasted with the high theology of later growth which came to be attributed to him. The sum and substance of all that is to be found in St. John is contained in the truth of God's Fatherhood, and his most profound and mystical verses are simply developments of the idea that we are children of God. Now the Sermon on the Mount is from first to last a lesson for the children. It has already been pointed out how every part of it is pervaded by this reference to the Father ; and though we do not say that even were this removed there might not remain a great deal of sensible and useful advice, it is certain that its whole character would be altered, that that would be taken away which at present binds or rather fuses all its parts together, and that some portions, and those not the least precious, would be utterly destroyed. To us it seems that not even when he spoke to Nicodemus about being born again, did he go further into the mysteries of religion than he does in the case of the golden rule, and that there is no precept in the Gospel of St. John which more urgently than this requires to be read in the remembrance that we cannot bear fruit except we abide in him.

XV

MEEKNESS AND GENTLENESS.

FORMERLY assailants of Christianity selected the supernatural element as the exclusive or chief object of attack, and there seemed to be a general understanding that its moral teaching was worthy of all acceptation ; now-a-days the latter is distinctly challenged, and some portions, which are undoubtedly characteristic, are categorically condemned. The passage beginning at the thirty-eighth verse of the fifth chapter of Matthew, in which occur these words :—" Ye have heard that it hath been said, An eye for an eye, and a tooth for a tooth : but I say unto you, That ye resist not evil: but whosoever shall smite thee on thy right cheek, turn to him the other also"—is pronounced to be exaggerated in tone and language, and to contain rules which are unworkable, and which, were this not the case, no man of sense or spirit ought to be expected to follow. The " meekness and gentleness of Christ" is thought to be a mistake.

It may readily be admitted that the words "resist not evil," taken by themselves and literally interpreted, enunciate a precept which cannot be strictly and absolutely followed. A literal and universal obedience to it would yield strange and disastrous results; it would establish a weak and cowardly temper, a poor-spiritedness, with which we should be sorry to see Christian poverty of spirit identified; it would give the rogues their own way, and make them masters of the world. Jesus himself did not follow slavishly any such rule, and the brightest pages of human history are those which tell how his people have resisted evil unto the death, and struck hard for truth and freedom.

But it does not follow that therefore Jesus was mistaken, or that Christian teachers, in adopting a more rational interpretation of his words, are guilty of paltering with truth, and resorting to strange shifts in order to escape from the plain meaning of their master's precepts. The way to ascertain the plain meaning of such precepts is not to isolate them and interpret them literally. The literal sense of words is not always their real sense. To insist upon it in the case of writings which are allegorical or poetical is to make nonsense of them ; and it is well known that the Scriptures abound in figurative language. So that it is quite illusory to speak of avoiding evasions and hair splittings, and sticking to the literal sense of language. It is precisely because we wish to ascertain the real meaning of the Scriptures that we must refuse to apply to every passage the literal method of interpretation. This adherence to the letter is particularly unfortunate in the case of Jesus, who, far from being a prosaic, matter-of-fact speaker, was one who loved the vividness of figure, and dared to employ the spur of paradox, and thought more of the spirit than the letter of any precepts, whether they were his own or proceeded from them of old time ; one who was not careful, as we moderns are obliged to be, to measure his words, and state all the limitations and modifications of a principle, but threw truth boldly and broadly on the hearts of men, to bear fruit where it should find congenial soil.

If, therefore, we decline in this and similar cases to be pinned down to a narrow and literal interpretation of Christian precepts, it is not because we desire to evade a difficulty, but because we want to hold by our Lord's real sentiments, which are certainly not by that means to be ascertained.

Jesus does not absolutely forbid his followers to resist evil. He forbids them to follow the ancient rule of "an eye for an eye, and a tooth for a tooth." That rule embodies the rude justice of retaliation and revenge; satisfies the natural desire to return blow for blow, the determination to let no man off without giving him as good as he brings, and to make my assailant suffer quite as much as he has made me;—and others besides the men of old time count that fair and lawful. That, Jesus undoubtedly forbids; distinctly and absolutely, without reserve or qualification, he forbids his people to resist evil for the sake of resistance, and to gratify a spirit of revenge.

That is a different thing from self-defence, and opposition to evil for wise ends, and in a generous and self-sacrificing temper. All men are in some cases, and Christians more straitly than other men, bound to resist evil. The history of this world is the history of a long conflict between good and evil; and to this conflict all honest men are called, and particularly all who name the name of Christ. It is the duty of every man not only to take all lawful means to protect his own life and property, but, as occasion is presented, to defend the weak against the strong. It is the duty of every community to suppress disorder and to punish wrong-doing ; of every nation to repel wanton aggression, and to fight to the death, if need arise, for its interests or honour.

But it is a duty which need not be discharged in a spirit of hatred and vengeance ; and where duty is not in question, these passions are not to be indulged.   Instead of them the spirit of meekness and gentleness ought to rule. This is the doctrine of Jesus, by which we are not ashamed to stand ; and which we maintain to be neither unpractical nor unmanly. It would be silly and cowardly to adhere literally to the practice of turning the other cheek to the smiter ; but it is wiser and braver to bear a blow than to nourish hatred and seek for revenge. We shall certainly not tamely surrender our possessions to the first rogue that sets up an unjust claim, which would be to commit a three-fold wrong,—to him, to ourselves, and to the community ; but we may believe that the less we have to do with litigation the better, and that gentle methods are generally the best, and we are certain that a meek and quiet spirit is an ornament above price. The mere robust virtues, the courage of the masterful Roman which he named virtue or manliness, self-reliance, independence, and such like, are good and needful,—the Lord Jesus did not despise them, though he did not need specially to inculcate them ; but there are other virtues more congenial to his temper, of a rarer and higher strain, which did greatly need to be enforced, and which found their interpreter and champion in him.   These virtues of meekness, humility, and forgiveness are accordingly distinctively Christian, and no follower of Jesus must neglect them either in theory or practice. It is not against them that they are liable to be counterfeited, and that they easily run into vices which are unlovely in the extreme.   All virtues are liable to this : courage often borders upon rashness, and firmness degenerates into obstinacy ; and if the meanness which calls itself meekness, and the humility of hypocrites are peculiarly offensive, that is not to be charged against true gentleness and humbleness of mind. "*Corruptio optimi pessima ;*" and hatred of the 'corruption' must not damp our zeal for the 'best.'   True meekness is not unmanly.   Moses was not less truly manful because he ruled his own spirit ; and there is no lack of strength in the character of the meek and lowly Jesus himself.   True gentleness is not impracticable.   Let no one say that the law of Christ 'will not work.'   It will work ; and what is more, nothing else will.   The more violent methods of oppression and war have had a pretty fair trial and have not done much ; it is time that we should see whether it be not true that more is to be made of men by the way of gentleness than by that of revenge.   It is written both in the Old Testament Scripture and in the New that "the meek shall inherit the earth."   We believe this, because we believe that "the earth is the Lord's," and that "God is love."

XVI.

ALMS.

IN the course of the passage referred to in last chapter, Jesus says, "Give to him that asketh of thee : and from him that would borrow of thee, turn not thou away."

Very unsound, and even mischievous counsel, we are told, and that not by hostile critics only. And so it is—"in the letter." To give to every beggar is one of the most foolish things any one can do.

A great change is coming over public sentiment on this subject. It is a natural act of kindness to bestow alms. Our compassionate feelings are gratified, and in a simple condition of society real distress may thus be relieved and actual good done. It is the chief of Christian duties to love one's neighbour, to consider the poor, to do good as one has opportunity ; and almsgiving has been commonly accounted as a great part of practical Christianity. It is usually claimed as a glory or admitted as a redeeming feature of religion, that it has encouraged and promoted works of charity. We are now, however, beginning to doubt the wisdom of indiscriminate almsgiving. It is known that the practice of benevolent persons encourages imposture and improvidence, while it is more than suspected that its effect is to intensify the evils of pauperism and distress which it is designed to alleviate. Wise Christian ministers find it necessary to condemn the practice, and to entreat their charitably disposed hearers not to give to any one that asks them, unless they know something of the case, and are satisfied that their bounty will be wisely used. In most of our larger cities and towns, societies have been organized for the systematic relief of the poor; and the old practice of putting the hand in the pocket and giving money to "objects of charity," instead of being looked upon as a virtuous act, is resented and condemned as an offence against society. All which is somewhat bewildering to old-fashioned people. They think it is against the teaching of their Saviour; they refuse to believe it; they hold that they cannot be wrong when they at the same time gratify a compassionate impulse, and obey an express command of Christ. And others, knowing that those things are true, and not sorry to get something against religion, join in the cry which is waxing louder daily, that Christianity is effete, or, as they express it, "played out;"— not only its miraculous elements being discredited, but its simplest and most distinctive precepts giving way before the march of intellect and the spread of modern light.

What are the facts? That Jesus teaches to love our neighbour, to be kind and helpful, to do for him the best we can ; and that teaching this to an eastern people, in a poor country with a very simple civilisation, and expressing himself, as was usual with him, sharply and vividly, he said, "Give to him that asketh of thee." Does it follow from this that he is to be quoted as approving, nay, as enjoining, careless, indiscriminate, and essentially lazy and selfish giving in present circumstances ? No indeed : and, on the contrary, if it can be shown, as shown it has been, that by that method Christian people are doing harm to the poor themselves, they are bound to pause, and to seek some more rational and effectual method of keeping Christ's law. His command is to bear one another's burdens, to do good; and in condemning indiscriminate giving, we simply condemn an illusory and formal obedience which is practical disobedience, and claim that the law shall be obeyed in spirit and in truth.

Jesus lays down no rule as to the manner and method of giving. That is a question of administration to be determined by common sense and experience, which cannot be determined once for all, but must be settled with careful regard to the changing conditions of social life. It is now agreed by those who have knowledge and experience, that the old methods of administration are defective; people are plainly told that it is their duty to distrust the stories of beggars, and to resist the impulse to buy off painful importunity by the gift of sixpence; they are warned that if in this lazy fashion they indulge a merely selfish benevolence, they must not flatter themselves that they are doing good; in other words, they are taught that by this plan they are not keeping, but breaking, Christ's commandment. If we would fulfil his law and walk in his steps, we must not merely be ready to put our hands in our pockets and send a mendicant away because she crieth after us; we must think, and plan, and take some trouble in order really to do good. For those who will do this—as many are now trying to do—there is a splendid field which may be expected to yield great results. It is a sad feature of our industrial civilisation, under which so astonishing prosperity is enjoyed, that while wealth accumulates at one end of the social scale, poverty and squalor, and disease and crime, grow at a frightful rate at the other. The poor we have in abundance, and it is the pressing question of the time how they are to be treated. The poor-laws, well meant and perhaps indispensable, are, as at present administered, a fruitful source of pauperism, and are regarded by many friends of the poor with distrust and aversion. Few would now advise that the poor should be handed over from private charity to a system of legal and compulsory relief. Rather is the conviction spreading that there is need of more sympathetic action; of a more painstaking system of personal helpfulness and brotherly kindness. It is perceived that there is a work to be done which money alone cannot do; that the rich must go down and meet the poor, and become acquainted with their wants, and bring to bear

upon them the power of a personal sympathy.
And what is this but an acknowledgment that
the law of Christ is right after all, and that it
is only on the lines he has laid down, only in
the spirit he communicates, only by the efforts
of men and women who are ready at the cost
of some pains and sacrifice to obey his law,
that this sore evil under the sun is to be removed or allayed ?   Chalmers made a splendid
beginning in Glasgow in a former generation,
and showed what might be done.   Our associations for relieving distress are doing a good
work amongst us now, which deserves the
support of all Christian people ; and if the
church of Christ would deserve well of society,
it must set itself with enlightened zeal to take
the lead in this, the great work of the day.

XVII.

SELF-DENIAL.

THERE is no room for mistake as to our Lord's meaning, when he said to Peter and the rest of the apostles, "Do not come after me unless you can deny yourselves and take up your cross." They must be ready to leave home and friends, to be hated by their countrymen, and persecuted by their rulers, to give up their cherished opinions and hopes, to renounce their natural desires, to endure hardness, and, if need be, to die for his sake and for the gospel which they should preach in his name. That is what he meant, and what, as the history tells us, they had actually to do.

But reading it as we must read the sentence, "If any man will come after me, let him deny himself," as a general law of the kingdom of heaven, are we to understand that no man can be a true Christian unless he in like manner breaks off natural ties and separates himself from the world, and gives himself to the preaching of the Word ?   So it has seemed to many. Self-denial in early times came to be identified with asceticism, and the sad countenance which Jesus condemned to be accepted among his followers as an appropriate sign of piety.   Now that that view has fallen into disrepute, and the opposite principle of living in the world a blameless and useful life has obtained currency, it is sometimes alleged as a reproach against Christians that they have thrown overboard one of the cardinal principles of the doctrine of Christ. 'You are only make-believe Christians,' it is said ; 'you profess great loyalty to Christ, but you take good care to set aside his most characteristic precepts ; you live exactly like other people, and deny yourselves nothing in particular ; whereas, if you were in earnest, you should sell all you have and give to the poor, and occupy yourselves wholly with heavenly things.'

Fully admitting and even urging the necessity of a more general and thorough obedience to this and other Christian precepts, we cannot allow that those who make this charge, any more than the ancient ascetics, take a true view of the matter.

We distinguish between the circumstances of

the apostles and our own. To say nothing of special mission and exceptional gifts, the attitude of society in general, and of the ruling powers in particular, was then such that a faithful profession of discipleship to Christ almost inevitably entailed persecution. The same thing has repeatedly happened in the history of the church —in the first centuries, for example, when Christians were required to offer sacrifice to the deity of brutal emperors; after the Mahomedan conquest, when the faith of Islam was forced upon subject races at the point of the sword; at the time of the Reformation in many lands, our own among the number: and we cannot say that the same may not happen again. We may also be tolerably certain that in private life occasions will present themselves, when, for conscience sake, earthly ties may have to be sundered and earthly prospects ruined: and without boasting, it may be asserted, that among the followers of Christ there exists sufficient devotedness to meet any such crisis, public or private, in a fashion worthy of the best days of Christian heroism; that there are men and women, not a few, now living, who are doing far harder things than it would be to confess Christ before persecutors, and suffering for duty and for love's sake sorer pains than the sharp but brief agony of the stake.

But the society in which we move, the government under which we live, are not hostile to religion.   Our world may not be very strictly orthodox or enthusiastically religious, but it rests on Christian foundations, owns rules and customs which have been moulded in accordance with Christian ideas, and treats the profession of Christianity with so much respect that men are more tempted to affect a religious habit which they do not love, than to conceal religious principles which they cherish.   And although this does not by any means abrogate the law of Christ, or take away all opportunity of practising self-denial, it certainly shows that our cross, in outward respects, is different from that which our Lord and his apostles had to bear.

Further, we must see that we understand what is the principle of self-denial.   It is not recommended because God delights in pain, or because there is any holiness or virtue in sorrow. Jesus himself came eating and drinking, sharing the life of his time, tasting such of its good things as were offered to him, enjoying the company of friends, avoiding danger when he could do so without neglecting the work his

Father gave him to do; and he certainly did not go out of his way to find disagreeable experiences, or afflict either body or soul. It was his lot to be a poor man; he went about preaching because that was his vocation; and he was crucified because in speaking the truth he made powerful enemies who resolved to put him out of the way.

So he teaches us to live purely and simply, to be content with what we have, and do our duty; bids us be cheerful, and kindly, and courteous, and put away needless care. He forbids us to be of a sad countenance that we may appear unto men to fast, and indicates with sufficient plainness that there is no virtue in putting on a melancholy face that we may appear unto God to fast. There is not a word of his that encourages asceticism, or suffering for suffering's sake. It was because he knew that in an evil world tribulation must come, that in evil hearts there are desires which must be repressed and rooted out, that in common life men of brotherly spirit must suffer affliction for others, and bear their neighbours' burdens, that he urged so strongly the necessity of self-sacrifice. Not for itself, but for the ends it serves, did he recommend it. Practised for its own sake, it is mere self-righteousness of a sorry type, and very easily becomes a very dark superstition.   Practised for the truth's sake, in order that by sacrificing one's own ease or inclination others may be blessed, it is the highest strain of virtue, which brings as its exceeding great reward a thorough sympathy with the Master, and a share in his joy.

This principle once grasped, an end is put to such unworthy questionings as one sometimes hears :—What must we deny ourselves ?   What may we lawfully use ?   They are seen to be away from the subject, and are at once put aside.

The rule is—*First*, absolutely to deny " ungodliness, and worldly lusts, and to live soberly, righteously, and godly ;" *Secondly*, to deny ourselves whensoever and howsoever we are required by the supreme law of love so to do.

It is on this ground alone that we can entertain the question of the lawfulness of private property, and the necessity of absolute renunciation.   It is recorded that on one occasion Jesus expressly ordered an inquirer to sell all that he had and give to the poor, but it does not follow that he requires this universally. That was a test, a hard test, designed for a special case ; and there is no general precept.

He knew the man with whom he had to do, and saw that this was the only way to save him from trusting in uncertain riches and losing his soul, and enough of the circumstances is apparent to enable us to understand and approve his dealing ; but before it can be established as a general principle, that rich men must always "go and do likewise," it would require to be shown either that this was necessary for their own good, or that it would really help the poor and promote the well-being of society. If this can be clearly made out, then may the rich be called upon, in the name of Christ, to put their possessions into a common fund. If in this or any other way we can help our neighbour, we are bound to make the sacrifice. If it is brought home to any man's conscience that in this way he ought to serve his Master, that man's course is clear. But the opinion of the wisest men— an opinion confirmed by the general course of history and the fate of various experiments— at present is, that such renunciation would do more harm than good ; and therefore Christians are not only entitled to refrain from it, but bound to seek some better way of fulfilling their Master's law. Christianity is not communism ; it is not identified with that or any form of social organisation ; it deals with other things. As a form of social organisation, communism has not hitherto commended itself to general acceptance ; and meanwhile, instead of renouncing property and luxuries, men are wise to study to be quiet and do their own business, and do good as they have opportunity, and accept the task, in many respects higher and harder than renunciation, of using their riches as stewards of the bounty of God.

The country is at present agitated on the temperance question, and earnest men, shocked and alarmed by the manifold evils of drunkenness, are calling upon Christian people to give up the use of intoxicating drink altogether. Those who take time to speak rationally on the subject make this demand, not on the ground that drinking is in itself an evil or a sin, but that abstinence is an act of self-denial necessary as a protest, an example, a help to weaker brethren. So stated the appeal is a strong one, which it is very hard sometimes to resist. If it were certain that the method is a wise one, no Christian could refuse to give it a trial ; but this is precisely where the teetotal case breaks down. That a man who cannot drink in moderation is better not to drink at all ; that people who cannot afford to clothe and educate their children, or insure their lives, or save a little for bad times, have no right to waste money on whisky; that in society men might very profitably drink less wine, and both men and women refrain from all occasional doses of stimulant — these and the like counsels of prudence need no argument. Further, that if it is to be a help to the tempted, we should put some restraint on lawful and safe indulgence, and, if necessary, banish wine for a time from our tables, the least instructed Christian is fully aware; and many Christians do this without thinking it necessary to make public proclamation of their self-denial. But there is no virtue in abstinence itself, any more than in celibacy; and when it becomes, as it readily does, a source of pride and uncharitableness, it is a positive evil. Temperance is an absolute duty; abstinence is not; and before abstinence can become, as some zealous people would like to make it, a term of Christian communion, it must be conclusively established that it is a necessary means to a good end, that it is hopeless to teach men self-control and rational temperance, and that only by total abstinence is society to be saved. There are many who think so and say so, but they have not as yet pursuaded men who take a large and moderate view. When they can do this, they may be assured that there are not wanting men and women, as full of love, as capable of sacrifice, and perhaps not less humble than the zealous, but not always temperate, advocates of abstinence, who, as we have heard a veteran and much-honoured abstainer say of his non-abstaining brethren in the ministry, "would not for a moment think of allowing a mere fleshly appetite to come between them and the souls of their brethren."

Our "cross" consists in those trials which come to us in the course of God's providence—those sacrifices, not made for their own sake, which the welfare of others or the cause of duty entails.

> "We need not bid, for cloistered cell,
>   Our neighbour and our friend farewell;
>   Nor strive to wind ourselves too high
>   For sinful man beneath the sky.
>
> "The trivial round, the common task,
>   Would furnish all we ought to ask—
>   Room to deny ourselves, a road
>   To bring us daily nearer God."

Of this law love is the fulfilling. Within the sphere of natural relations it is well understood,

and mostly well obeyed, by all whose natural
affections are fresh and true. When these are
sanctified by Christian principle, then is self-
sacrifice to be found in its beauty and its
power. To be found, not always to be seen
and known ; for it loves retirement, and shrinks
from applause. In many quiet circles, all
unknown of men, unsuspected often by those
who are near and dear, unappreciated by
those for whom the sacrifice is made, are meek
hearts bearing the cross and seeking no reward.
These the Father, who seeth in secret, knoweth
and doth reward abundantly ; and if, per-
chance after they are fallen asleep, the record
of their virtue leaps to light, even selfish men
feel their hearts swell within them as they read,
and from this sinful world there rises a chorus
of warm praise which bears witness how deeply
this law is rooted in the hearts of men.

XVIII.

FASTING.

JESUS treats fasting as a recognised religious exercise. He does not enjoin it—and the same may be said of prayer and the giving of alms,—he takes it for granted, as in existing circumstances he could hardly have failed to do, that persons who made any pretensions to the religious character would fast ; and in the course of his warnings against hypocrisy and ostentation, he bids his disciples take care not to make a show of their prayers, their almsgiving, or their fasts. In another place he mentions it, along with prayer, as a means of strengthening faith. On one occasion the Pharisees, having asked him why his disciples omitted this practice, drew from him a very important declaration of his views. There can be no doubt that this disregard of fasting was a serious innovation in the eyes not only of the disciples of John and of the Pharisees, but of many of the best disposed in Israel, an innovation not less serious than laxity on the subject of Sabbath observance appears to the religious world at present. His reply would be anxiously awaited both by friends and foes. As a reply it is a fine example of the skilful frankness which made him dreaded as a disputant; but we are more concerned with it as a weighty deliverance on a great question of the religious life. "Can the children of the bride-chamber fast while the bridegroom is with them? As long as they have the bridegroom with them they cannot fast; but the days will come when the bridegroom shall be taken away from them, and then shall they fast in those days." Here we have the supremacy of heart-religion broadly asserted, and the liberty of individual conscience in matters of an external kind completely vindicated. It is assigned as a satisfactory reason for his disciples' conduct, that they were not in a fasting mood; and it is implied that he would neither bid them fast for fasting's sake, nor prevent them from fasting in other circumstances if they should be so inclined.

Fasting is, therefore, certainly not of universal obligation. It is not necessary to salvation. It has no virtue or merit in itself. No man nced think to please God by wearing a sad countenance, or by giving himself pain or discomfort. No such marvellous and degrading conceptions have any place in a true Christianity. On the other hand, it is open to any person who finds fasting beneficial as a personal discipline, to use it privately and without self-righteous display.

There can be no doubt that, setting aside its superstitious observance, fasting has occupied a great place in the history of religion, and that many good men have valued and used it as a means of spiritual benefit; and it is by no means certain that it deserves to be treated, as it often is in this country, with contempt. We may rejoice in the healthy sentiment which repudiates the attempt to revive the mediæval practice of fasting as a meritorious action, a means of procuring the favour of God; but we must not so readily conclude that there is no ground for the use of this discipline as a means of personal edification. Those who know how widely it has prevailed will be inclined to believe that it has some foundation in human nature; and, from regard to the holy men who have testified to its benefits, will be anxious to understand the matter, and so to qualify themselves intelligently to use their Christian liberty.

In the simplest view, then, which we can take, it appears that fasting is a natural result of strongly excited feeling, especially when it is of a painful or melancholy kind. When one is under the sway of absorbing emotion, the wants of the body are sometimes forgotten, and its appetites suspended for the time. It is often difficult to induce persons who have given way to excessive grief to take necessary sustenance. The annals of mysticism, in India and elsewhere, are full of instances of the extraordinary physical effects which are produced by intense spiritual excitement. And, without going so far, no one who considers the tremendous issues which religion raises, and the intensity of the emotions which it inspires in those who are truly awakened and brought face to face with God and the great questions of eternity, will find it difficult to understand how temporary abstinence from food should have early become associated with the access of strong conviction or profound penitence.

Further, it is a familiar fact that abstinence from all but what is barely necessary to support life is often conducive to bodily health, or requisite for the cure of disease. Men of the better stamp, also, perceiving the need of governing the flesh and bringing it into subjection, have judged that as a body pampered by surfeits and dainties becomes the home of divers lusts and fiery passions, so a wise temperance may help a man to overcome temptations by which he may be assailed.

Men have found, besides, that by observing such temperance they rendered themselves more fit to sustain severe mental exertion, or to engage in spiritual meditation. Literary men, who wanted to keep their brain clear, or to endure an unaccustomed strain upon their mental faculties, have sometimes been careful, if not to fast literally, at least to restrict themselves to a very spare diet, which is frequently all that fasting amounts to even in tolerably strict ecclesiastical practice ; and spiritual men, the more especially when luxury has waxed wanton, and drunkenness has prevailed, have often had recourse to a similar practice as a means of qualifying them for devout studies and special prayer. "Fasting," says Jeremy Taylor, "if it be considered in itself, without relation to spiritual ends, is a duty nowhere enjoined or counselled. But Christianity hath to do with it as it may be made an instrument of the Spirit, by subduing the lusts of the flesh or removing the hindrances of religion." " He that undertakes to enumerate the benefits of fasting may, in the next page, reckon all the benefits of physic ; for fasting is not to be commended as a duty, but as an instrument, and in that sense no man can reprove it or undervalue it but he that knows neither spiritual arts nor spiritual necessities." To this may be added the testimony of a Scottish saint. To the charge preferred against him of contemning fasting, this answer was returned by George Wishart :—" My lords, I find that fasting is commended in Scripture ; therefore I were a slanderer of the gospel if I contemned fasting. And not only so, but I have learned by experience that fasting is good for the health and conservation of the body. But God knoweth only who fasteth the true fast."

Apart, then, from ecclesiastical ordinance, and above all superstitious abuse, this ancient and widely-spread practice stands on its own foundation in the nature of man, and vindicates itself as a bodily means towards mental and spiritual ends. Thus, and thus alone, is it recognised by Jesus. He does not command it ; he lays down no rule : but he does not forbid it ; he only insists that it be not observed superstitiously and ostentatiously. If, as appears to be the case from the language of Scripture and the testimony of eminent Christians, it is useful as a personal discipline, it may be so used according as every one shall find it necessary or convenient. A church is not justified in imposing it on all its members as necessary to salvation, and is hardly wise even to recommend it to all and sundry at any specified time ; but any church is entitled to recommend it to the consideration of its members for private use, as a means of promoting pureness of heart and increasing spiritual grace. And, lastly, fast or no fast, sad countenance or cheerful, it is the duty of all to rule their bodies with temperance, to flee fleshly lusts, and to give diligence that spirit, soul, and body be preserved blameless before God.

XIX.

PRAYER.

As with fasting, so with prayer ; it is uniformly treated by Jesus as a part of the religious life. But it is much more honoured, both by his own practice and by the frequency and character of his references to it.

As we have already had occasion to observe, he rests the practice of prayer upon faith in the Father ; and his first recorded utterance regarding it is in the form of a caution that it be sacredly kept between the soul and God. Christians are not to make a show of prayer like the hypocrites. We have to think of the habits of the east in order to understand the necessity of such a warning. At the hour of prayer a Mussulman makes his prostrations wherever he may be, and in whatever presence. In the parable both Pharisee and Publican go up to the temple to pray. It would suit the purpose, therefore, of a hypocrite to pray standing at the corners of the streets ; the multitude, seeing him so doing, would honour him as a very pious man. It is not customary in this country for men to perform their personal devotions in such public fashion. It is a ready way to acquire a reputation in certain circles to stand at street corners, but it must be in the way of evangelistic effort. And perhaps, on the whole, in the existing state of public opinion, there is more danger of our being deterred by fear of others from praying when we ought to do so, than of our doing this to be seen of men.

In all this there is nothing against, but everything in favour of, family and public prayer. A special encouragement is offered to united supplication, and the practice of common prayer is bound up with the history of religion everywhere.

We are also warned not to use vain repetitions. We have to distinguish between much speaking and much praying. We are not to repeat the same thing many times, and spin out a long address as if there were virtue in the length of a prayer or the number of times it is recited. We are neither to use, nor ourselves to become, praying machines. But we are to be instant in prayer, to ask again and again, as the poor widow clamoured for justice, or the neighbour at midnight for bread,—to ask in the assurance that we are speaking to a Father who, more than any parent upon earth, loveth to give good things to his children. This is the secret of our Lord's view of prayer. It is a child's pouring out of penitence and petition to the Father in heaven.

In certain aspects in which God presents himself to our minds, he appears as one to whom prayer is useless or impossible. Belief in an Infinite Being, who has foreordained whatsoever comes to pass, however it may be logically necessary, is difficult to bring into a workable relation to personal religion, as Calvinists know well. Indeed, no logical answer has been given to the query:—If God has ordained all things, what is the use of my asking him? It passes into a region where thinking breaks down—a region into which Jesus does not lead our thoughts. He speaks of the Father, knowing that, once the reality of that relation is felt, the question of prayer becomes one, not of metaphysic but of spiritual instinct, and the language of prayer the natural and irrepressible utterance of the soul. Prayer is with him not a doubtful expedient for influencing a deity seated apart in light inaccessible, certainly not an attempt to impose our will upon the Almighty, and disturb the working of his unchanging laws, but the utterance of a child's trust and desire—his agonised, it may be, but still submissive and trustful desire. "Father, if it be possible, let this cup pass from me : nevertheless not my will, but thine be done."

It deserves to be particularly remarked that so far from thinking God's foreknowledge, in which preordination is in the case of an Infinite Being involved, an obstacle to faithful prayer, he adduces it as a positive encouragement. Whereas there are some who say, "If God knows already what I want, where is the use for my asking ? if he is going to give it, I shall get it without praying ; and if not, my prayer will not make any difference ;"—Jesus says, "Be not like the heathen, who use vain repetitions; because your Father knoweth what things ye have need of before ye ask him." If the thing we ask be needful, we shall get it ; and if it be hurtful, we certainly shall not. He will give us of things good and convenient exceeding abundantly above all that we can ask or think, and will not give us anything bad though we cry for it ever so loudly and long : and they are happy who pray in this trust, verily believing that God will send what is best for them, and place them where it is best for them to be; who are able when some of those things which we pray to be delivered from—as pain, disappointment, or bereavement—come upon them, to say, 'This, too, is from the Father, and is of the things I had need of, though I knew it not.'

Another thing in connection with prayer, to which Jesus attaches the utmost importance, is the necessity of a merciful and charitable spirit in the suppliant. We need not think to pray unless the heart is right with God, and the heart cannot be right with God unless we are, as far as lieth in us, at peace with men. " Blessed are the merciful, for they shall obtain mercy." " If ye forgive not men their trespasses, neither will your Father forgive you." He even puts this into his brief model of prayer, teaching us to say, " Forgive us our debts, as we forgive our debtors," so making us, as it were, name and consent to the condition of our own pardon. It is clear beyond any doubt that, according to the Lord Jesus, we need not say, " Our Father in heaven, forgive us our debts," unless we are ready to add, " as we forgive our debtors."

It commends itself to a natural sense of

justice that persons who will not forgive others should not themselves be forgiven, and to this sentiment there is made in one of the parables a very plain and powerful appeal. Forgiveness of a debt already granted is revoked in consequence of the debtor's cruel treatment of a fellow-servant indebted in a small sum to him ; and we acknowledge the justice of his punishment. We cannot but feel that there is something frightfully incongruous when a miserable sinner, bent on vengeance and full of ill-will, makes his prayer for pardon at the footstool of God's throne. We know, moreover, that we are helped or hindered in our own trust and comfort in prayer by the presence or absence of a forgiving spirit, and are the rather encouraged to ask mercy for ourselves when we are enabled from the heart to forgive others. Our prayers are hindered when we are in a bad humour. We may join in acts of prayer, may repeat words of supplication, but we cannot sincerely say, " Our Father, forgive our debts," unless we are able to add, " as we forgive our debtors."

If, further, we understand the exceeding evil of revenge and hatred, and reflect that nothing can so effectually separate us from God and frustrate all his good purposes concerning us, as an unforgiving spirit; if we consider that it would be the greatest curse to us if God were to permit us to cherish such a spirit, and is indeed inconceivable that we should enjoy the blessing of forgiveness while we continue in one of the worst of sins; it will not appear extravagant to say, that we dare not ask our Father to forgive us our debts, without also asking for grace to forgive our debtors.

When ye pray, be not as the hypocrites; be simple, be persevering, be trustful, be merciful; be instant in prayer to your Father which seeth in secret;—thus may be summed up the teaching of Jesus on the subject of prayer.

When his disciples asked him to teach them to pray, he replied by telling them the story of the importunate friend, and repeating to them the " Our Father," which has become the common prayer of Christendom. Criticism of this venerable and precious form seems almost profanation. It occupies a position unique and supreme. It stands above the course of controversy, apart from the wrangling of sects. Suiting all modes of thought, falling naturally into every language spoken among men, it has brought throughout the Christian centuries its gracious message to the children of God, and

borne again to heaven their purest aspirations.
It is part of the public worship in almost all
churches ; and to those of us who believe in
the communion of saints, and who like to feel
ourselves in sympathy with many of our fellow
creatures, there is no part of the service of the
sanctuary that is more dear.   When one thinks
how many sects celebrate a separate worship,
and how many congregations expect from their
pastors, and not always in vain, glorification of
their own peculiar tenets, and assaults on those
of their neighbours, it is pleasant to know
that so many meet on the sacred ground of this
simple prayer, and in spite of our foolish rivalries
testify to the unity of the Spirit by the universal " Our Father," which we utter at a throne of
grace.

There are in this prayer the elements of true
religion, those broad principles with which Jesus
loved best to deal, and which lie deeper than
the currents of intellectual disputation and the
turmoil of ecclesiastical feuds.   It is so simple
that it falls easily from the lips of a child ; it
is so deep that great thinkers and holiest saints
have testified that they can have no higher
spiritual desire than that they might be able to
use it with increasing sincerity.   The more its

preface is pondered, and its petitions studied, the more are we constrained to feel how true it is; how it hangs together; with what strong grasp it seizes the realities of religion; how close it lies to the great duties of life and dictates of conscience; how it rebukes all superstition and all double-mindedness, all unbelief and hypocrisy; how securely it guides our feet upon the earth, and how graciously it lifts up our hearts to heaven.

Lord, have mercy upon us, and incline our hearts to pray this prayer.

XX.

WORSHIP.

In the important matter of public worship, Jesus conformed to established usage. He went to the synagogue on the Sabbath day. He attended the great feasts in Jerusalem, and made his offering in the temple. His last evening was spent in eating the passover. But he set little store by matters of form, and taught that in worship as in life the great thing is "spirit and truth."

The churches in this country have of late been greatly troubled concerning this matter. In England the progress of the mediæval reaction in favour of vestments and practices which are symbolical of high sacramental doctrine, has raised a controversy that goes near to rending the Established Church to pieces; the aid of Parliament having even been invoked, and an Act passed, as some think hastily, for the better regulation of public worship. In the northern part of the island things have not reached such a pass, but what has taken place is nowise more creditable to modern Christianity. It has been a burning question in General Assemblies whether congregations shall stand or kneel when they pray. Leading churchmen of various denominations have made it a matter of conscience to oppose the introduction of instrumental music in the service of public praise. This is truly discreditable. In the superstition of Christ's bodily presence in the sacrament, bad as it is that men calling themselves his disciples should follow it with Bibles in their hands, there is still some substance; and it has the venerableness of antiquity, and the sanction of imposing authority and wide acceptance: but the Scottish controversies about postures and organs want a serious foundation of dogmatic conviction to make them respectable, and are so alien from the general sympathies of Christendom as to sink to the level of a parochial squabble. On such questions there is room for difference of opinion; they are questions of arrangement which must be discussed and settled by the majority of voices; but when men raise them to the first magnitude and discuss them as if they were vital to religion, then one must wonder that

they can venture to do this in assemblies con-
vened in Christ's name. It is deplorable to
hear a disciple of Christ speak as if it were a
matter of conscience whether the psalmody
should be led by a single voice, by a choir, or
by a harmonium : one remembers what Jesus
used to say about the men who made broad
their phylacteries, and wonders what he would
think of disciples who, in the name of an especially spiritual worship, thus magnify matters of
a carnal and accidental kind. Surely into the
counsels of such polemics the true disciple of
Jesus cannot enter. He may love the form in
which he has been reared, but he will not make
it an idol. He will love it so well as to wish
to see its blemishes removed, and to try to
improve it, as taste shall direct and prudence
allow ; and the only question of vital importance
in his eyes will be how far it tends to help or
to hinder faithful souls who would render their
homage to their Father in heaven.

It does not follow from the principle laid
down by Jesus, as it certainly is not suggested
by his practice, that churches are unnecessary,
and forms of worship out of place. Men are
not pure spirit ; inhabiting bodies, their spiritual
actions and feelings depend to some extent on

bodily conditions, and crave bodily expression. If you are to have common worship at all, you must offer it in some place, and both convenience and propriety suggest the setting apart of some place in particular : the general feeling must be uttered in some way so that all may understand and participate, and therefore some form, simple or elaborate, some common order, more or less seemly, there must be.

Neither does it follow, as some are ready to argue, that fine churches are a mistake, and a beautiful service wrong. It is not conclusive to say that no temple we can raise is worthy of God, and that it is foolish to think of suitably adorning our houses of prayer. As Solomon made confession, saying, " Heaven, even the heaven of heavens, cannot contain him," when he was dedicating the most splendid temple wealth could procure and art embellish, it is open. to those who believe most fully in the dispensation of the Spirit to serve their God with their best and fairest, and to wish to make their church buildings in some degree accord with their sacred use. Of another argument, often used in this connection, we may have something to say when we come to consider what the Master said to Judas about Mary and her box of ointment.

It does not follow from the principle of
spiritual worship that it is wrong in all circumstances to use elaborate ceremonial or even
symbolism.   Much as we may dislike the extravagances of the modern ritualistic school, we
must not allow ourselves to be driven into an
equally extravagant and uncharitable admiration
of simplicity.   In present circumstances there is
some danger that this may take place, that in
England evangelical churchmen, and dissenters
of all shades, may become more and more
narrow, and that the traditional Scottish sentiment against a liturgy and fine music may
be confirmed.   It is necessary, therefore, to remember that spiritual worship is not worship
destitute of order and beauty, or, to avoid even
the appearance of unfairness, worship reduced
to a bare and severe simplicity.   Simplicity has
a value and beauty of its own, and symbolism
has dangers only too well known ; but simplicity,
also, has its dangers, and even for symbolism
there is something to be said.   At all events,
those who are accustomed to a very simple form
are not entitled to suppose that therefore they
are true worshippers, and they certainly have
no right to judge that all high churchmen are
of necessity superstitious.   It may be conceded

that this very self-conceited, and, as Mr. Arnold would say, intensely " Philistine" opinion, has its good side,—the churches which follow the Presbyterian model have a grand history in which the simplicity of their worship is founded, and by that simplicity they have been saved from perplexities which beset communions of more stately ritual ; it may be admitted that they are wise not to handle it rudely, not even to improve it rashly : but it cannot be allowed that they should extol its defects, and sit in judgment upon others.

The solemn beauty of a cathedral service has a value of its own, higher perhaps than that of anything Presbyterian worship can show ; and the common Anglican worship appeals to modern taste and culture in a way which has told upon Presbyterianism in various ways, and has in no small degree been instrumental in stirring up its adherents to amend their defects. These defects no enlightened Presbyterian denies. He may be satisfied, indeed, that nothing better is to be desired than a well-conducted service after the ancient reformed order ; but he is not bound to admire the kind of worship which, widely departing therefrom, had come to be associated with the predominance of Presbytery.

In a church of mean design and furniture ; in cold, rambling, metaphysical, bombastic, or slovenly prayers, listened to, or not listened to, by so-called worshippers in all varieties of posture ; in praise which may have been sincere, but which certainly was horrible to a musical ear ;—it is hard to discern the charm or the value of Presbyterian simplicity : and when a service has degenerated into such a condition as used to be common and is not yet quite unknown in Scotland, it must be said that the church which tolerates it has wandered as far as it is possible to do from the ideal of Christian worship, has allowed a state of things as alien to genuine spirituality as it is easy to conceive.

If, therefore, there are dangers and disadvantages connected with elaborate services, let it be confessed that there are dangers incident to a system of simplicity and free prayer ; and let it not be forgotten that, as has been well said, " If there may be a superstitious reliance on forms and display, there may be an equally superstitious reliance on the want of them ; the one superstition being no way more respectable or sensible than the other."   It is bad to rely on any ordinance, and to bind up the grace of God in a sacramental system—

hardly any error seems to be so much at variance with the principles of the doctrine of Christ; but it is not good to be puffed up because of our freedom from such error, and to be bigoted either about form or the absence of form. True worship is spiritual, and for this reason is broad and tolerant, friendly to all that is lovely and admirable, ready to adapt itself to time and circumstance, and desirous to take to itself whatever it can of the beauty of holiness, especially when consecrated by the use and the reverence of many generations of pious souls.

XXI.

THE SABBATH.

IT is curious to find the Sabbatarianism of the
Pharisees so exactly reproduced in Puritan-
ism, and so obstinately retained by the successors of the Puritans. It is not only that
Sabbatarianism is so alien from the spirit of
the Master's teaching, and the liberty wherewith he maketh his people free ; but that this
was, in his own conflict with the Pharisees, and
in that of Paul with his opponents, so distinctly
emphasised. There are many parts of ecclesiastical doctrine which are without foundation
in the words of Jesus ; but it does not often
happen, as in this case, that opinions have to be
maintained against his express statements. A
large number of Christians—whole communities,
indeed—have been brought to hold, and to impose
upon society for generations, opinions regarding
the Sabbath, founded upon principles which the
Lord Jesus absolutely demolished ; and it is

not easy to understand how those who uphold such opinions can reconcile them with his teaching, or fail to see that if they are right his principles ought to be regarded as erroneous, and his practice condemned.

The Sabbatarian principle is this. God had made a certain demand upon men. As he required a certain portion of their goods, so also he demanded a fixed portion of their time. For his own good pleasure he made the demand. Six days of the week a man might have for his own works, but the seventh must be given to God. No matter what reason or necessity there might seem to be for working, he must abide by the letter of the law ; God had said it, and man must obey. This, not to speak of the puerilities of rabbinical tradition, is the Sabbatarian position in its proper form.

There are many even yet who will find in this statement nothing amiss. From the tone of recent discussions and of private conversations, it is evident that the ruling idea in this country still is, that the Sabbath is purely a positive ordinance, an act of homage prescribed, in fact, a burden imposed by the Great Taskmaster ; and the question is, on the one part, how to bind it as firmly as possible on the

country and in the family ; on the other, how to
make it as light as may be without coming
within the scope of divine penalties.   That it is
a blessing to the country, and to every inhabit-
ant thereof, as to which we ought all of us to be
diligently contriving how we and our neighbours
can enjoy it best and get most good from it, is
a view which comes forward far too rarely, and
when it is put forward receives far too scant
sympathy.   Yet it is the Christian view ; it is the
Lord's view; a view, be it observed, asserted by
him, not as to the Christian Sunday or Lord's
Day, which some hold to be an institution
altogether different from the ancient Sabbath,
but to the Jewish Sabbath itself.   "The Sabbath
was made for man, not man for the Sabbath."

Believing as firmly as his adversaries that the
Sabbath was ordained by God, and knowing the
Father as he did, he could have no doubt that it
was intended to be, not a burden, but a blessing;
and he had the ancient Scriptures themselves
distinctly on his side.   For it is not fair to
charge the absurdities of Sabbatarianism upon
the religion of Israel.   There are two versions
of the fourth commandment.   In the one the
reason annexed runs thus : " For in six days the
Lord made heaven and earth, the sea, and all

that in them is, and rested the seventh day: wherefore the Lord blessed the Sabbath day, and hallowed it." There is nothing very tyrannical in that. It reads as if the Almighty appointed for men made in his image a law analogous to that which he followed himself. There is a divine work and a divine rest, therefore let man work and let him also rest. God blessed the Sabbath day, not cursed and blighted it, but blessed and hallowed it, set it apart that every man in Israel might securely enjoy its blessedness. That certainly bears out the maxim of Jesus that the Sabbath was made for man.

Another version of the commandment is given in Deuteronomy, and in it this is the reason assigned :—" That thy man-servant and thy maid-servant may rest as well as thou. And remember that thou wast a servant in the land of Egypt, and that the Lord thy God brought thee out thence through a mighty hand and by a stretched-out arm : therefore the Lord thy God commanded thee to keep the Sabbath day." Is not this really a humane, a tender sentence to occur in a code of laws ? The Israelite is enjoined, in the name of the great Deliverer of his nation, to see that his servants as well as he enjoy the boon of rest. He is to think of his fathers' bondage and of their deliverance when he is told to keep the Sabbath day. Here is not a hard taskmaster binding heavy burdens on men's shoulders, but a God who cares more for men than they would for themselves, who has compassion on the slaves, and for whose divine regards even the oxen and asses are not too mean. And this is written in the law. Whatever be the true history of the Pentateuch, both Exodus and Deuteronomy were received by all parties in Jerusalem as sacred and authoritative. The Pharisees had these things before them when they blamed him for letting his disciples rub a few ears of corn, and for healing a man on the Sabbath day. Said he not justly that they made the commandment of God void by their tradition?

However it came there, there it stood, and there it stands, bearing witness that this is the true and original idea of the ordinance. It was a holiday, and a holiday secured beyond all encroachment or change. Six days the weary slave must be at his master's call, to fetch and carry at his master's bidding, to toil for his master's profit, his time not his own but his master's; but on the seventh, a higher voice is heard, which even the master must obey,

" Let him alone ; he shall do no work to-day. Remember how thy fathers were slaves in Egypt ; let him rest to-day as well as thou ; and come, both thou and he, and rejoice in the Redeemer of Israel."   On the ground, therefore, of Scripture, nay of that very " letter " of the law by which the Pharisees, ancient and modern, so strongly hold, he is right and they are wrong. He fulfils the law ; they are for making it void, emptying it of its true meaning, turning it from a boon to a hardship, from a blessing to a curse, from a token of God's kindness fit to draw his children's hearts to him, into a means of making healthy men and women, and especially young men and maidens, fear and loathe his service and his very name.

For the various illustrations which the narrative affords of the application of our Lord's principle, readers are referred to their own recollections, which they may profitably refresh. For the present it must suffice to establish his principle, and to insist upon it as the guiding one in all questions regarding the Day of Rest which are raised in our time.   It is an ordinance designed for the good of the community, and especially for the bodily and spiritual refreshment of the children of God ; and it is the business of Christian people to yield to it an enlightened reverence, to commend it to the acceptance and respect of society, and to welcome and further all arrangements, even though they should give some shock to old prejudice and require some change of habits, which tend to subserve the great end of making this institution more extensively and thoroughly available for the good of man.

Into the controversy concerning the obligation of the fourth commandment, and the change from the seventh to the first day of the week, we are not required to enter here. It does not for me possess the importance which it seems to have for many, and it is not raised by anything which Christ said on the subject. Call it what men will, this is an institution which Christians are bound to uphold, not as against society as is too often assumed, but in the interest of society; an institution which, if it were used fearlessly and faithfully in the spirit of Christ, might be more of a blessing to the world than it is, and very much more than it is thought to be now. The great thing is to get away from the slavish negative view which is characteristic of Sabbatarianism, and to hold fast the truth as it is in Jesus, free, and positive, and rational;

to consider not so much what it is unlawful to do according to narrow traditions of men, but how we may best use the day for our own and others' good, in the light of common sense and piety. It is a sign of our backwardness in this matter as in many others, that we are so much more occupied with what we should not, than what we should do, thinking more of "abstaining from recreations," than of enjoying spiritual benefits. When one reads, as any one may do, in books and tracts of good intention, that many a course of sin may be traced to taking a walk on the Sabbath day, or hears persons condemned for performing music in the family circle, or thinks of poor children forbidden to play, and constrained to sit wearily reading books which may be good but are certainly not lively, or with folded hands to listen to the not uniformly pious or interesting talk of their elders ; when one remembers the ideas, the densely superstitious sentiments, prevalent and active in society,—ideas and sentiments which are indeed giving way, but not before religious so much as secular influences,—one blushes to think how we have made void the doctrine of Christ by puritanical traditions, and have gone back, not even to the weak and beggarly elements of the law, but to perversions and corruptions of the law, since it is not from Moses but from the Pharisees that such things come.

"The Sabbath was made for man."

We need a day of rest, need it more than ever it was needed before, inasmuch as we work harder and live faster than men ever did upon the earth. Instead of defending this institution with bated breath, we ought to proclaim it as the privilege of the people, and especially of the sons of toil, and bid them regard it as a God-sent blessing, and do all we can to ensure that it shall be enjoyed by as many as possible as a day of rest and innocent recreation, of refreshment of body, mind, and spirit. Absolute rest we cannot all have, some of us being obliged to work that others may rest and be refreshed ; but the majority may and should rest from labour and relieve the tension of the mind. It would be out of place to discuss details, but at this juncture it may be well, even out of season, to avow one's delight in seeing city-bred artisans breathing fresh air and looking upon the strength of hills and the loveliness of flowers, and one's hearty sympathy with those who would throw open parks and galleries to those who have no gardens and pictures of their own, and cannot enjoy such things on any other day of the seven.

We need a day for public worship and spiritual edification. To the spiritual man there is no special sacredness in any time or place. He 'regardeth not the day.' But he does not therefore undervalue a means of grace so venerable and important. He is glad when it is said to him, Go up to the house of God ; he rejoices in the day God made for him; he is thankful to belong to a community of whose life public worship forms a part, and which by the most sacred sanctions preserves a day on which the sound of labour is hushed, and the cares of business are suspended, and the distractions of sport and pleasure are put aside, so that in quiet and comfort he can meditate on the things that are unseen, and go up with his family and neighbours to the house of God to offer his praise and prayer, and to receive some cheer and comfort for the battle of life.

We need, moreover, a day for doing special Christian work. Most of us are too much occupied during the week to be able to devote as much time as might be desired to direct endeavours to advance the good of our neighbours, and for this many value the leisure of the Lord's day. Such work is true rest for the spirit, and it is strictly in harmony with the Master's teaching and example to do it on the Sabbath day. It is indeed one of the most cheering signs of the times that this kind of actual Sabbath observance is gaining ground— that every Sunday the Lord looks down upon so many earnest men and women in town and country, who spend the day, not in indolent ease or selfish meditation, but in genuine Christian work, and that he is leading so many to use its opportunities in such wise that it promises to become in the future, even more than in bygone days, a blessing to men for whom it was made.

XXII.

OATHS.

THE custom of swearing and making vows
rests on the idea of invoking God as a faithful
witness to the truth of words spoken or engage-
ments made, and appealing to him as supreme
judge and avenger in case of transgression. It
has been widely prevalent, and was, in various
forms, distinctly recognised under the old covenant. It was said by them of old time, " Thou
shalt not forswear thyself, but shalt perform unto
the Lord thine oaths." Jesus says, " Swear not
at all ; neither by heaven, for it is God's throne :
nor by the earth ; for it is his footstool : neither
by Jerusalem ; for it is the city of the great King.
Neither shalt thou swear by thine head, because
thou canst not make one hair white or black.
But let your communication be, Yea, yea ; Nay,
nay : for whatsoever is more than these cometh
of evil." It would seem that in the miserable
fashion of the time, men sought to indulge a

license of swearing without breaking the letter of the law, as if, because the name of God was not uttered, the oath might be used without irreverence and broken with impunity ; and this sorry transgression Jesus forbids. He says, " Swear not at all."

It thus appears that he had something else in view than that curious and most unlovely practice of cursing and swearing in common talk, which has in our time happily disappeared from decent society, and is heard only from the lips of drunken fools or among the very dregs of the population. How common the habit was we know from many stories of a former generation ; we see it in old plays, where the conversation of gentlemen is freely garnished with oaths and curses ; we gather it from old sermons, which are full of lamentations and rebukes. Barrow puts forth all his strength to assail it, and even in his honest indignation at its mingled wickedness and senselessness loses something of his stately calm. To say that Barrow has devoted a sermon to the subject is to say that it is most ably and exhaustively discussed, and to refer the reader to a magazine of information and argument. If the evil could have yielded to reason or eloquence, it must have been demolished. There is nothing more remarkable about the habit, however, than its want of meaning. It is difficult to see wherein consists the satisfaction which, presumably at least, it yields to those who indulge themselves in it. And this quality, too, has not escaped his notice, but is thus exposed by him in a sermon on "Offending in word:" "This offence is particularly most inexcusable, in that it scarce hath any temptation to it, or bringeth with it any advantage, so that it is unaccountable what (beside mere vanity or perverseness) should dispose men thereto. It gratifieth no sense, it yieldeth no profit, it procureth no honour; for the sound of it is not very melodious, nor surely was any man ever preferred for it or got an estate thereby; it rather to any good ear maketh a horrid and jarring noise; it rather produceth displeasure, damage, and disgrace. Wherefore of all dealers in sin the swearer is apparently the silliest, and maketh the worst bargains for himself, for he sinneth gratis and selleth his soul for nothing. An epicure has some reason, and an extortioner is a man of wisdom compared to him; for they enjoy some pleasure, or acquire some gain here, in lieu of their salvation hereafter. But he offends heaven and abandons happiness, he knows not why nor for what; a fond humour possesses him, he inconsiderately follows a herd of fops, he affects to play the ape—that is all he can say for himself. If men would but a little consider things, surely this scurvy fashion would be soon discarded, much fitter for the scum of the people than for the flower of the gentry; yea rather, much below any man endued with a scrap of reason, not to say with a grain of religion."

It is commonly assumed that an exception is to be made in favour of public and solemn oaths, as those which the Sovereign takes on being crowned, or a witness before giving evidence in a court of justice. It is even an argument used by Dr. Barrow to reprehend rash and profane swearing, that it weakens the sanctity of an oath, on which in great measure the welfare of society depends. Others, however, as the Society of Friends, take a different view; and although we may not agree with them in supposing that there is anything absolutely wrong in conforming to the custom of the country, it certainly appears that they are right in thinking that even public oaths are included in this "Swear not at all."

It is true that we must not be slaves to the

letter. It is also true that public oaths are not explicitly referred to, and that the prohibition might only extend to private speech and conduct. We should not impugn an ancient and venerable custom on the narrow ground of the letter of this commandment. If the letter only had been in question, and if strong ground of expediency existed for maintaining public oaths, we should not press these words any more than others in the sermon. But it seems that public swearing, equally with private, is against the spirit of the law, and it is extremely doubtful whether the continuance of the custom is justified by its serving any good end ; and therefore, although, while it is the custom and law of the land, I make no scruple of compliance, I believe that it ought to be discontinued.

What is the ground of this prohibition ? It is not merely that it is unseemly and irreverent to call in the great name of God on every light occasion,—"to take it," as the third commandment expresses it, "in vain." It is the principle that a Christian's "yea" or "nay" is quite sufficient ; that he should have such a regard for truth that the sanction of an oath adds no solemnity to his statements, no security to his promise. There is no real distinction between falsehood and perjury, since he always speaks as in the presence of God, and regards truth as the most sacred of things. There are no degrees in truth ; a lie is a lie whensoever and howsoever it is uttered ; and a Christian is careful to tell the truth in his simplest communication as much as when he is under the most tremendous oaths. These are for him, therefore, quite unnecessary. He can have no objection personally to call God to witness, if he is required by competent authority and in suitable circumstances so to do : but he cannot but regard the ceremony as altogether superfluous, and even offensive, as far as he is concerned; and he may consider that it is to be regretted that it should be imposed upon him in a Christian community.

It is indeed difficult to see the force of the arguments by which Christian divines support the existing practice. It is not to the purpose to say that it is desirable " to induce witnesses in a court of justice to apprehend themselves greatly obliged to discover the truth according to conscience ;" " to engage men to discharge public offices and perform the trust reposed in them ;" " to furnish competent assurances between man and man concerning the integrity, fidelity, and constancy each of the other ;"

"to tie men to the obedience due to their governors with strictest bonds of allegiance." Doubtless it is good to lay, in these and the like instances, the highest obligation upon the conscience. But why should an oath be necessary? Is anything wanted in addition to the obligation which every Christian acknowledges to tell the truth always and absolutely? And is it wise to uphold in this manner a distinction of obligation, and to institute a greater and lesser kind of falsehood? These are the questions raised by the words of Jesus, which it would seem to be difficult to answer with reference to persons supposed to be Christians.

But it is said there are nominal Christians who cannot be trusted, and we need oaths for them. It is true there are many nominal Christians whose word is not of much worth, and if the use of an oath be really effectual in terrifying such persons into veracity, this would go far to justify its retention. But it is more than doubtful whether it is of such avail. If oaths are by such persons held in awe, it is probable that it is more on account of the temporal penalty attached to their breach, than of the prospect of that dread judgment which they invoke. I write under correction, but it is my conviction that in general a man who will tell a lie will swear to a lie if he can do it with safety ; and that, for all practical purposes, oaths might be safely dispensed with, were the same punishment extended to falsehood deliberately uttered which is now awarded to perjury.

There remain those who are not Christians even by profession. Of these, some doubtless are amenable to the merely superstitious influences of awe and terror to which an oath appeals ; but the larger number, in all likelihood, regard them with entire indifference.

Admitting, as the testimony of experienced magistrates obliges me to do, that there is something in the argument from expediency in favour of solemn and public swearing ; there are, on the other hand, various considerations telling against it, which can only be indicated here. There is, for example, the injury done to the general feeling of reverence in the community by the irreverent associations connected with this ceremony and the manner in which in criminal courts it is often performed. There are the scruples of some Christians who believe that they cannot comply with this custom without breaking their Master's command. There is the case, too, of atheists, whose veracity no one would think of calling in question, and whom we have no right to put in the position of having their testimony rejected, unless they will use a formula which is to them empty or offensive. Chiefly in this connection it deserves to be considered whether it is wise to recognise a distinction between falsehood and perjury, between a man's word of honour, or rather his bare word, and his declaration upon oath ; whether the State would not do better for its own ends if, by abolishing such distinctions, and showing respect for the yea and nay of an honest man, it bore witness for the sacredness of truth, and raised the general standard of reverence for it throughout the community.

In conclusion, the position here maintained on the religious question may thus be stated : All swearing in public or in private is against that reverence for truth which ought to fill the children of God. A man's simple word is sufficient, and nothing more should be required. We are not obliged to refuse to take an oath when required by the law to do so ; there is no essential harm in it, and we are not slaves to the mere letter of our Lord's words. As long as our rulers enjoin it, we need not scruple to swear. But in a Christian country the greatest tenderness ought to be shown to those who have conscientious scruples, and when these are expressed, a simple statement should be received. And we should desire and endeavour that such enlightenment of conscience and regard for truth should be diffused throughout the community as will effect the ultimate and entire abolition of swearing on all occasions, as well of a public as a private kind.

XXIII.

FAITH.

How it came to pass that the strange idea took
root in the minds of men, that salvation de-
pended on holding orthodox opinions on religion,
it would take too long to tell.   It is not difficult
to see that it would suit the Church of Rome
to encourage such a notion, and there is enough
of the spirit of Popery in Protestantism, especially (for extremes meet) among the straitest
sects of that persuasion, to account for the
tenacity with which this notion is held among
ourselves.   There is no doubt that this is a
current conception regarding faith.   A great
many sincere people amongst us are firmly persuaded that what they have to do in order to
be saved, is to bring their minds to acquiesce
in the theology of their sect, to stifle doubts,
to distrust inquiry, and to count those who
cannot or will not accept the orthodox creed
as enemies of the truth and heirs of damnation.

And thus to persons of more active intellect than that possessed by the majority of respectable believers, the good news of God has been made to seem a hard thing, or at least coupled with hard and monstrous conditions. For it is mostly, as is now becoming generally known, a purely intellectual question, what creed a man shall receive. Different men have different ways of thinking; and notably on the profound and difficult matters embraced in ecclesiastical formulæ there has always been a great variety of opinion. Augustinianism and Pelagianism, Calvinism and Arminianism, are not, as their respective adherents have thought, representative of truth and falsehood; but exhibitions of different sides or aspects of truth which commend themselves to men of opposite philosophical bias, neither side having a monopoly of reason, or being exempt from the falsehood of extremes. That a man should be held to be morally culpable and subject to condemnation because his opinion leans to what, as being the view of the minority, came to be called heresy; that, for errors which may be due to unavoidable ignorance—errors arrived at in hard and conscientious study, and held in sincerity and all reverence, it may be in the very beauty of holiness and tender charity—a man should be adjudged to the pains of hell for ever, is a thing which has offered to many a serious difficulty, as being repugnant to what they have learned to believe of the justice and magnanimity, not to speak of the mercy, of God. We feel that we should be ashamed to do such a thing, even we who are evil ; and it is hard to believe it of our Father in heaven. There are many who refuse to believe that orthodoxy covers the multitude of sins, or that a man of blameless life, who cannot regard the Shorter Catechism as a perfect manual of divinity, or accept all the clauses of the Athanasian Creed, must "without doubt, perish everlastingly." The damnatory clauses in that Creed are indeed so grossly outrageous, that it is a marvel that they should have been endured so long, even in a church so patient and conservative as the Anglican. If the principle has not been so frankly stated in Presbyterian symbols, it is still more generally prevalent in the northern part of the island, and has more social power. Against it many now rebel, some with cool contempt, but others with bitter indignation. There are few causes which at present tend more to widen the breach between the intelligence of our country and its religion than this, that Christianity is identified with such opinions as to the necessity of accepting a particular dogmatic system, opinions whose only proper home is in the Church of the Syllabus and the Infallible Pope, and which Protestantism should cast out of its bosom for ever.

The faith of which Jesus speaks is not of this kind, as appeared in our remarks on Method, but must now be stated independently. Faith is trust ; a right attitude of the whole man, and especially the spirit that is in man, to his Father in heaven—a thing of the heart more than of the head ; and what is known in Christian theology as justifying faith is not acquiescence in this or that view of the doctrine of the Trinity or the Atonement, but loyal and affectionate trust in Jesus as the Son of God and Light of men, the Way, the Truth, and the Life.

It does not follow from this that one creed is as good as another, and that it is matter of indifference whether or not we are well instructed in the matter of religion. No one who has studied history and knows what power of widespread mischief lies in every religious error, no one who knows the pricelessness of true wisdom, will maintain that. On the contrary, if, instead of putting the belief which rests upon instruction and inquiry in the place of faith in God, we regard it as an indispensable means of attaining thereto, we can hardly attach too much importance to it or give sufficient diligence to acquire it. Those who are most liberal on this point will always be most anxious to have themselves, and to disseminate in the community, sound and enlightened opinions.

There is, moreover, a certain submission to authority, a respect for the general consent of Christendom, which is seemly and prudent. We cannot allow any doctors or any church to impose opinions upon us, and forbid us to doubt or search for ourselves ; we cannot resign the right, we dare not neglect the duty, of being fully persuaded in our own mind. The name of Athanasius himself, so unworthily associated with extreme orthodoxy, reminds us that a man may sometimes have to hold fast his convictions alone against a world. But, on the other hand, only a foolish conceit will despise the fact that an opinion is held everywhere and by all. That potent " spirit of the time," whom we all so much admire, and some of us with trembling, would be nothing the worse if he were somewhat less convinced of his own superiority, and more prone to believe that there was wisdom in the world before he arose. There is an intellectual arrogance that is full of danger, and a pride of independent judgment that can only be condemned. It is a good thing to remember the extreme difficulty of theological thinking, good not to be wise in our own conceit, good to reverence the forms of sound words which have nourished the piety of many generations, good to lay to heart the maxims of Holy Writ— that a sincere desire to do the will of God is the best qualification for knowing his doctrine, and that it is to meek and quiet souls he loveth to show his way.

Understanding faith in the right way, we can see why Jesus must have required his disciples to believe, and declared that only those who did believe could have everlasting life. It does not fall in with our present task to speak of personal faith in him as a Redeemer; but obviously, if he is a Saviour, we must trust in him, otherwise he is no Saviour to us. Keeping to that faith which he demands as a teacher, it is plain that he, like all teachers and prophets, must want first of all to induce people to believe what he says, and that unless and until they do so, they cannot get any good from him, or be

his true disciples. He came with a message
from God—the message that God is light ; and
he commanded men everywhere to repent and
forsake darkness and evil-doing and come to
the light. He declared the Father, who is love ;
and invited men to return to his love and service, that they might be delivered from death
and condemnation, and become, not in prospect
but in fact, heirs of everlasting life. He never
taught, as some do in his name, that his Father's
love is dependent on the faith of men, and that
unbelievers have no share in his paternal regards ;
he bids us believe in the love of the Father, and
so, not as a reward of faith, but by faith, in the
act of faith, "enter into," "lay hold upon,"
"have" eternal life. How could he do otherwise ? What is light if we have not eyes, or
will not open them ? What is even the love
of God if we close our hearts against him ? If
it is foolish to preach the gospel, as the church
has often done, in terms of threatening,—forcing,
as it were, her dogmas upon men on peril of
damnation ; it is wise, and indeed necessary,
that one who cometh with the good news of
God should beseech men to believe the news,
and be reconciled to him.

Yes ; but after all, was not Jesus somewhat

peremptory?   Said he not that he that rejected
his words should be condemned?   Did he not
wind up the Sermon on the Mount with a tremendous sentence upon those who should hear
his words and not do them?   Is it not a strong
thing for any teacher to denounce those who
would not receive him, as persons irrevocably
doomed to destruction?   How does this consist
with tolerance or with charity?   How does it
differ from the course taken by the churches,
which we have condemned?   What, in short—
for to this it comes, since we cannot deny the
fact of peremptoriness—is there in the teaching
of Jesus to justify the confidence and urgency
of his demand upon the faith and obedience of
mankind?   The ready answer of course is,
Because he came from God and spoke in his
name; and it is a true answer, though not
quite in the sense in which it is often understood.   But it is met by the further question,
How are we to know that he came from God?
and the common answer, Because he wrought
miracles, though it might convince Nicodemus,
will hardly be accepted as conclusive now.   The
miracles themselves require a great deal of
proof, and meanwhile the word of Jesus will
brook no delay.   Besides, there are many things

which no miracles, though they were wrought before our eyes, could make credible or worthy of acceptation. And this is not the argument used by Jesus himself. Beyond all doubt he appealed to the testimony of his works, but he did not rely chiefly, or even to any considerable extent, on their testimony. He claimed that his words should be received because they are true, and the proof of their truth he found in the heart and conscience of man. Coming from God with a message to men made in his image, he was sure that it must meet with a response from every honest and good heart. Conscience, which is the voice of God within, answers to Jesus speaking without ; the word in the heart confesses the Word made flesh. " If any man hear my words, and believe not, I judge him not ; for I came not to judge the world, but to save the world. He that rejecteth me, and receiveth not my words, hath one that judgeth him ; the word that I have spoken, the same shall judge him in the last day."

That is the position of Jesus, described in his usual luminous and comprehensive way. He judges no man, but the word judges all. He who so tenderly ministered to doubting Thomas can have no sympathy with, and is not responsible for, the judgment pronounced by Christians on honest sceptics. It is only of wilful rejection of truth approved by the conscience that he speaks in so strong terms. We who would learn of him must respect honest. opinion ; while we condemn unsparingly, and most of all in ourselves, the "evil heart of unbelief," the want of faith, whose root is in love of sin. We must distinguish between the monstrous growth of scholastic divinity, and the truth as it is in Jesus ; between the faith which consists in agreement in opinion with Aquinas or Calvin, and that which consists in trust in God and obedience to those laws of godly living with which the word of Jesus mainly has to do : and so be able to tolerate and even welcome difference of opinion, while we are intolerant of sin against light.

At all events, the word is the judge, now and always, and we may know that it will judge us at the last day, by the way in which we feel that it judges us now. It was because he knew assuredly that it judged his hearers as they heard, that he warned them of the condemnation which they braved. It is because his word is accompanied by the verdict of conscience, that, reverencing it ourselves, we venture to challenge for it the faith of the world. When one shall come to show us yet a better way, to set forth with greater plainness the chief principles of good living, to commend them with greater attractiveness, to enforce them with more powerful motives, him will we hear. If one shall come and shall reveal to us more and higher truth concerning the things that are unseen, and give us a better and more comfortable idea of him in whom we live and move and have our being, him will we hear, and him will we follow. But meanwhile, though many are going away from following Jesus, we are fain to say with Simon Peter, " Lord, unto whom can we go but unto thee ? thou hast the words of eternal life."

XXIV.

REST.

THE word care is used in two senses : it means
thoughtful and painstaking attention ; it means
also anxiety or trouble of mind. It is in the
latter sense that Martha is reproved for being
"careful and troubled about many things," and
that the apostle Paul exhorts to "be careful for
nothing." In the former sense carefulness, so
far from being against religion, is by it distinctly
required. Nothing that the Lord Jesus says is
to be understood as against a wise diligence
and forethought. "Take no thought for the
morrow" seems to encourage improvidence ;
but even if he had said this, we might have
remembered his vivid manner, and understood
these words in the same way as we understand
"If any man hate not his father and mother."
But the fact is, that our translators have needlessly increased the difficulty of the passage, by
thus rendering a word which means, "do not

be anxious," or, as some prefer, "be not distracted,"—exactly the same word which is used by St. Paul in the passage referred to, and which is translated "be careful," in the sense of "full of care" or "troubled."

This is wholesome counsel. There is a certain amount of thought and care which must be given to our worldly business, which if we do not give, to-morrow will find our affairs in sad confusion; we can hardly take too much pains to do our work well, or exercise too much foresight and economy in the management of our affairs. But this we may do without troubling ourselves with unnecessary anxiety. And it is not by the really useful trouble and labour which the struggle for existence demands, not by the measures of prudence which we are required to take, that men's hearts are burdened and women's nerves unstrung, but by our own fears, forebodings, and self-tormentings. By these, at least, chiefly. Care is not altogether of our own making, since life is full of difficulty and trial; but it is self-caused far oftener than most people are accustomed to think. Many of our anxieties are very much due to ourselves; and of those that are externally induced and inevitable, many are, by the way we cherish them, made heavier than they ought to be.

Is it not true that a great deal of the uneasiness and positive unhappiness of life is unnecessary? Do we not weary ourselves by anticipating troubles which never come, wondering what we shall do in difficulties which never arise, dreading dangers which turn out to be far less formidable than imagination represented? Do we not often make far more of real cares than they deserve or require, and fail to lighten them as we might by various means? Some are more prone to this than others, for it is a matter in which temperament has much to do ; but it is to some extent a general failing, and it is a great thing to know that we are commanded to dismiss such anxieties, that they are not to be nursed and brooded over, but resisted and overcome.

We are to consider that over-anxiousness serves no good end, no end indeed whatever, but to make ourselves and others miserable. When we have made the best arrangements in our power, and done all that we can, it is not good to anticipate results, and forestall disappointments. Anxious persons commonly allow this, saying, "We know it does no good to fret, but we cannot help it;" and it may seem, therefore, to be of no avail to use this argument. Still it is true, and with reasonable persons it ought to have weight, that the indulgence of such superfluous thought not only does no good but inflicts upon themselves and others a totally needless pain.

But we must quote the Lord's own words, which are, even among his words, of singular beauty. " Behold the fowls of the air : for they sow not, neither do they reap, nor gather into barns ; yet your heavenly Father feedeth them. Are ye not much better than they? Which of you by troubling himself can add a cubit to his life? And why take ye thought for raiment? Consider the lilies of the field how they grow ; they toil not, neither do they spin : and yet I say unto you, That even Solomon in all his glory was not arrayed like one of these. Wherefore, if God so clothe the grass of the field, which to-day is and to-morrow is cast into the oven, shall he not much more clothe you? O ye of little faith?" Have not these words a singular charm, a delicate poetry and suggestiveness, which gives them a power beyond their mere logical force? Their argument is plain, and does not need to be drawn out here ; but there is more here than argument from less to greater, more than " you are dearer to God than birds and flowers."   That is the great thing— trust in God, and of that we shall speak.   But we seem also here to feel the power that is in fresh air and green fields,—the message of the flowers, the soothing influence of nature, which, as helps to banish care, are by no means to be despised.   Many who cannot analyse their feelings, and to whom Wordsworth is a weariness, know that a walk in the country has often lightened their cares.   Men, neither religiously nor sentimentally inclined, make their escape from their offices, and, going out to the hills near their city, find relief from the tension of business by drinking in the beauty of plains and streams.   Students, when the strain of reading and speculation becomes too great, find it good simply to go out and sit in the sunshine, and listen to the prattle of a brook, and watch the birds building their nests.   And there is more in this than the mere benefit of fresh air and exercise, mighty healers as these are of body and mind ; for nature has a message to the spirit that is in man, and exerts a healing power ; and they hear this message with true profit, and feel this power with added efficacy, who learn with Jesus to find God in nature, and let the birds and the lilies speak to their hearts of him.

The substance of what he says, however, is in this : "Your heavenly Father knoweth that ye have need of these things :" it is foolish and worse to trouble yourselves about them ; it is heathenish, pardonable in the Gentiles who knew no better, but unworthy of those who believe in the Father in heaven. As unbelief is the real cause of care, trust is its proper cure,— trust and resignation. "Cast thy burden on the Lord, and he shall sustain thee." "Come unto me, all ye that labour and are heavy laden, and I will give you rest. Take my yoke upon you, and learn of me ; for I am meek and lowly in heart : and ye shall find rest unto your souls. For my yoke is easy, and my burden is light."

It is necessary, for the right understanding of these much prized words last quoted, to get quit of what it may be feared is the general impression—that the yoke here spoken of is that of obedience to Christian law as given by Jesus, his burden that which he imposes upon his followers ; and that this yoke or burden is said to be light and easy as compared with certain other yokes or services to which men have

submitted, as that of sin, or of legal righteousness.   This is quite away from the mark, and
introduces an idea of the easiness of Christian
service which is foreign to Scripture, as might
without difficulty be shown ; but it is sufficient
for our purpose and more pertinent to point out
that it is exegetically wrong. 'My yoke,' as has
been pointed out by Dr. Robertson of Glasgow,
in his posthumously published *Sermons and
Expositions*—a work far too little known, but
greatly prized by those who have studied it—is
not the yoke I lay upon you, but the yoke I
myself carry, 'my burden' the burden I bear ;
just as ' my peace ' is the peace I enjoy, or ' my
joy ' the joy which fills my soul.   The yoke is
his Father's will, in doing which he found delight ; the burden the same will, in submission
to which he found rest to his soul amid all the
disappointments and sorrows of his career.
Therefore he says, " Take my yoke and"—not
obey me, which would suit a yoke of his ap-
pointing, but " learn of me ; for I am meek and
lowly," learn to bear your burden meekly as I
bear mine.   Moreover, speaking not merely as
a teacher, but as a fellow-sufferer who had experience of that which he recommends, he adds,
" And ye shall find rest unto your souls : for

my yoke is easy and my burden is light," which
latter clause means, as will now be seen—not
as is most unworthily represented, " I will not
be so hard upon you as the rabbis" but—" my
yoke is easy to me, and my burden feels light ;
I have in meekness and lowliness found rest
unto my soul."

Perhaps it is because these verses are in our
Bibles marked off as a separate paragraph, as
they certainly ought not to be, that so little
attention is commonly paid to their connection
with what goes immediately before. If the
reader will only begin at the beginning of the
foregoing verse, and read straight on, he will
perceive that the secret of the peace which Jesus
professed to enjoy was in his knowledge of the
Father, his continual enjoyment of filial fellowship, his unclouded faith in the righteousness of
the Father's purpose and the might of his love ;
and that it is by communicating this knowledge,
and giving men power to become sons, that he
offers to give them rest : which is in perfect accordance with the principles of his doctrine, and
describes the only way that rest can be given.
Rest of soul is an inward thing, and is not to
be had by other than inward means. It is
not by being taken out of the world or delivered

from the ills that flesh is heir to ; not thus, by any means, that we are taught to seek for rest. It is the foolish thought of the carnal mind, that all that is wrong with us comes from without, that if we could only get rid of certain embarrassments, and procure more congenial employment, and be placed beyond the reach of certain temptations—if, in short, things were otherwise than God has seen fit to order them, we should be cheerful, contented, happy. "O that I had wings like a dove, for then would I fly away and be at rest." But we cannot fly away ; most of us, at least, are well tied down to our place and our duties, and must take things as we find them. And though we could always fly away from our post, we should not be at rest, for new places would bring new troubles, and in every station we should find something to chafe us and try our temper. The secret of unrest is within, in the discontented spirit, the unbelieving heart ; and the evil must be met there. Let us learn to do the duties and bear the ills of life in the spirit of Jesus, carrying with us the ornament of meekness and quietness, and we shall not care where we go or what may befall us, but shall, like the man of sorrows with the meek and lowly heart, find rest unto our souls.

"O God, who alone canst order the unruly wills and affections of sinful men ; Grant unto thy people, that they may love the thing which thou commandest, and desire that which thou dost promise ; that so, among the sundry and manifold changes of the world, our hearts may surely there be fixed where true joys are to be found."

XXV.

TRUST.

WHILE trust is thus prescribed as a cure for cares and fears and vain forebodings, it is not presented as a substitute for labour and foresight. It is charged against the teaching of Jesus that it has a tendency to encourage a visionary and idle temper, and to intensify the improvidence and recklessness which are among the sorest evils of our time. Unfortunately zealous Christians often speak and act so as to merit this reproach, alleging the authority of the Master ; and thus, as so often, he is wounded in the house of his friends, and his name brought into contempt. It is really wonderful to hear the language which some people use about trust in Providence. It is supposed to be a wise and pious thing to encourage early marriages among the poor. If two foolish young people, who have not enough between them to furnish decently a single room, and have parents dependent upon their support, choose to get married, there are always good people at hand who, instead of chiding them for their selfish recklessness, look upon them with sentimental sympathy, and actually admire and praise them because they show such "trust in Providence." It is not long since we read that these views found utterance in that Economical Section of the British Association for the advancement of Science, where so many unscientific notions are ventilated. In a discussion on Statistics and Population, a violent attack was made on the doctrine of "prudential checks;" grave and presumably sane men publicly declared that the poor should be encouraged to obey natural instincts and put their trust in Providence; and the statement is reported to have been greeted with applause by the assembled votaries of science. Possibly this was given in mere ignorance, and for sentimental reasons; but more probably it was called forth by the supposed piety of the opinions. The public were glad to hear in those halls of science an appeal to Providence. It was as if, in the department of biology, some one had stood up against the Darwinians for an orthodox creation of species; it was Religion *versus* Science, and religion got the cheer. Which is not in itself a thing to be regretted. It is to be regretted, however, and that bitterly, that such nonsense should be identified with Christianity, and supposed by many to receive special support from the teaching of Christ. It has already been shown that the words which are supposed to countenance these views have nothing whatever to do with the subject. They condemn unnecessary anxiety, and inculcate boundless trust, but they do not absolve from the necessity of exertion and of prudence any more than the prayer, "Give us our daily bread," absolves from the duty of labour, or the other petition, "Lead us not into temptation," makes watchfulness unnecessary. The advice given there is perfectly rational, its beauty and power to soothe being hardly more remarkable than its homely wisdom and sanctified common sense. We need not go over the ground again, but refer the reader to what is said in last section, or rather to the passage itself—it is in the end of the sixth chapter of Matthew; its encouragement of recklessness, he will find, is only in appearance, and that is due partly to mistranslation, and partly to neglect of the point of view.

It may be worth while, however, to devote a

few sentences to this curious notion of trust in Providence. If those who use such language were accustomed to analyse their ideas, they would find that it really amounts to an expectation of miraculous intervention. Their words, at all events, have no meaning, unless they point to the over-riding of natural laws, and superseding of natural efforts ; and thus they nourish, in ignorant people, expectations which are vain ; and encourage them in a superstition, practically akin to that of the Italian peasant, who expects the intervention of his patron saint or of the Virgin Mary.

It is not necessary to maintain that God cannot do what is thus expected ; it is not necessary even to assert that he will not : it is sufficient to allege, as matter of fact, that he does not ; as matter of faith, that there is nothing in the way of promise, which warrants any one to expect that he will. This world is governed under fixed laws, which it is our interest, and indeed our duty, to discover ; and when discovered, to obey. Whether we know these laws or not, the forces of nature work inexorably. If a man walk into the midst of a fire he will be burned, and that without regard to his madness or sanity, his badness or goodness, his infidelity or faith. If he leap into the air from the top of a tower he will fall to the ground, and the amount of injury he shall sustain depends on something other than the capricious interference of the Most High. In the case of well-known natural properties, as of fire, stone, water, and laws like that of gravity, this is well known ; and no people are so foolish as to defy such laws, and trust to God for deliverance from the consequences. That we call tempting Providence.

But there are laws which are more complicated and less known, in whose region superstitious piety finds scope. As, for instance, the laws of health. Impressions still linger that sickness is sent under the direct and mysterious control of Deity. These are fostered by the real ignorance which prevails, by the apparently mysterious manner in which, in a district or family, one is taken and another left, by cases of extraordinary cure or unexpected recovery, by the mystery which surrounds the principle of life. It is not common to find people who refuse to take medicine, though occasionally, persons, who most properly call themselves Peculiar People, expose themselves to penalty for neglect and refusal, because they think it their duty to trust entirely to God. But if the public now generally believe in, and use, means of cure, they are only gradually coming to understand means of prevention. It is not many years since a prime minister of this country scandalised the religious world by venturing to suggest to the magistrates of a certain city, devoutly asking a national fast on the approach of pestilence, that it were well that they should look to their drains. We are coming now to see that the counsel was wise and not necessarily impious ; and to own that without care and effort, in this as in other cases, prayer is a mockery and an impiety. It is no longer possible to ascribe the results of our neglect to the visitation of God, or to ask him to avert fever from people who breathe foul air, and drink foul water, and live in general defiance of all sanitary law. To neglect known precautions, such as vaccination, ventilation, cleanliness, disinfection ; to rush needlessly into infected houses, and take no care to prevent contagion,—is not courage but sheer folly, not trusting but tempting Providence, not piety but with those who know what they are doing, sin.

Is it really different when people set at naught economical laws and prudential considerations ?   And if not, why should it be thought a right thing to encourage imprudence on the part of the poor ?   It may be supposed that a confused notion that every birth is the result of a direct act of creation, and that therefore no responsibility rests on those who are instrumental in bringing human creatures into the world, has something to do with such mischievous opinions.   So at least it would appear from the marvellous maxim that Providence always sends meat where there are mouths to be fed, and the indignation which the doctrines of Malthus arouse.   But it is inexcusable that men, however misled or confused, should come forward and give such counsel to the poor ; especially men who take very good care to act on other principles themselves, having, it is to be hoped, a good balance at their banker's, and being almost certainly tolerably well insured ; who, if they heard of young people in their own family circle marrying without funds or reasonable prospects, would not regard them as objects of admiration or models of pious confidence.   Why should it be thought a right thing for poor people to be less prudent, who have so much greater need ?   Why should it be considered a friendly thing to give them such advice ?   And why, above all, should it be deemed a pious thing to bid them act thus, trusting in Providence ?

" Trusting in Providence," forsooth ! It would be more exact to say, trusting in the Poor Laws, which do step in to rescue the victims of improvidence, and therefore are a fruitful source and careful nurse of pauperism, and a serious obstacle, as at present administered, to the well-being of the working-classes.   Their true friends should tell them, as the more intelligent among them already know, that there is no privilege like what Burns calls the glorious one of being independent, and no way of being independent but by prudence and self-control.   They should tell them that what is spent by the drinking members of their order upon intoxicating liquors would more than suffice if applied in the way of Benefit Societies, or Government Annuities, or Savings Banks, to raise them out of poverty and provide for sickness and old age ; and that no man has a right to indulge in strong drink or any other luxury who cannot afford to " provide for his own."   They who are zealous for God should teach that he will not be found on the side of selfishness and improvidence ; remembering that an apostle has said, " If any provide not "—and provide is foresee, look ahead, and procure supplies—" for his own, and especially for those of his own house, he has denied the faith, and is worse than an infidel."

Having said so much as to what trust is not, let me here, without going into the subject at large, indicate certain things which are certainly included in its scope. We may trust absolutely in the constancy of natural forces and uniformity of natural laws—a greater thing than trusting that the course of Nature and Providence will be interrupted constantly to please or to benefit the favourites of heaven. We may trust that God maketh all things work for good.

> " Behold, we know not anything,
> I can but trust that good shall fall
> At last,—far off, at last, to all,
> And every winter change to spring."

We should trust that God will pardon all our sins ; and this we should believe with the same undoubting faith we are wont to have in the light of the sun and the unchanging ordinances of heaven. We should always firmly trust that he will accomplish his high purpose, and make us perfect as he is perfect ; which is the last and highest reach of that trust the Lord Jesus seeks to inspire, embracing as it does in its wide sweep all other things. On this last point we may well ponder these fine remarks of Channing's : " For this good we may trust in God with utter confidence. We may be assured that he is ready and anxious to confer it upon us ; that he is always inviting and leading us towards it by his providence and by his Spirit through all trials and vicissitudes, through all triumphs and blessings ; and that, unless our will is utterly perverse, no power in the universe can deprive us of it. Such is the good (perfection namely) for which we may confide in God. God promises nothing else or less. We cannot confide in him for prosperity, do what we will for success ; for he often disappoints the most strenuous labours, and suddenly prostrates the proudest power. We cannot confide in him for health, friends, honour, outward repose. Not a single worldly blessing is pledged to us, and this is well. God's outward gifts, mere shadows as they are of happiness, soon pass away, and their transitoriness reveals by contrast the only true good."

XXVI.

FORGIVENESS.

IT is a noteworthy fact that so little trace is to
be found in the teaching of Jesus of that doctrine of atonement by sacrifice and satisfaction
of divine justice, which comes forward so pro-
minently in the Epistles, and in later times has
assumed a position of overwhelming importance,
casting into the shade all other portions of the
systems of theology. Granting that there is
nothing in St. Paul's writings positively inconsistent with the recorded utterances of Jesus, and
bearing in mind that it is rather with the person
and work of Christ than with his doctrine that
the idea of propitiation has to do, it must still
be acknowledged to be a curious fact that this
idea, which is now chiefly associated with his
name, receives so little notice from himself. So
little, I say, because there are some of his sayings which, in the light thrown back by subse-
quent theological developments, may, to persons

familiar with these, suggest the great idea of reconciliation by blood, and I do not wish to overstate : were I to speak merely of the impression produced on my own mind by study of the Gospels, I should say that in the words of Jesus taken by themselves, there is no foundation whatever for the doctrine of atonement as now commonly received. Leaving it to theologians to explain this, I note the fact here, to account for what to some may appear strange, that in dealing with our Lord's own teaching on the subject of forgiveness and salvation, I have nothing to say concerning any of the theories of atonement in which, to many, all truth on this subject is contained.

Jesus taught, as the prophets taught before him, without reference to sacrifice or offerings, that God is waiting to be gracious; that if sinners will forsake their ways and return to him, he will not fail to pardon abundantly. Whereas the priestly system rests on the idea that the chief difficulty is to appease the anger of God, the prophet proceeds on the assumption that it is in the unbelief and sinfulness of the human heart that the most formidable obstacles in the way of reconciliation are found. The priest draws up a code of ceremonies and prescribes burnt-offerings or penances; the prophet proclaims a message from on high, and seeks to touch the conscience of man. As prophet and teacher, Jesus delivers his message in his Father's name; uses every resource of argument and entreaty, in order to have that message received. That God will pardon penitents there can with him be no possible doubt; and he makes no mention of any consideration whatever in the shape of sacrifice or other means of satisfaction. He teaches with unequalled plainness and persuasiveness that pardon is sure. His way of uniformly treating this as a thing absolutely settled, hardly needing to be stated, to be constantly assumed, has something about it that is infinitely reassuring. As we learn of Jesus, there grows upon us the conviction of this truth, the habit of taking it for granted, the feeling that it is an axiom in the things of the spirit; not a thing which may reasonably be believed as upon the whole well supported by evidence, but which is above all shadow of doubt, firm as the throne of the Eternal, changeless as he knoweth no change. There are two conditions mentioned; first, of course, that the sinner repent and turn to God; secondly, that he be ready himself to forgive others—a wholesome condition, of which we have already heard something in connection with Prayer: but these complied with, the penitent may be assured that the Father will gladly hear him and receive him with joy.

It is not only from the general strain of the Saviour's teaching that this comfort is to be derived. The subject is expressly treated by him in the three parables reported in the fifteenth chapter of the Gospel according to Luke, which (thanks for once to the Pharisees) were drawn from him in defence of his consorting with publicans and sinners. The central word of that chapter is this, " There is joy in the presence of the angels of God over one sinner that repenteth." It is but a small thing to say that God is willing to forgive ; he longs to see sinners turning from their evil ways, and rejoices over penitents with exceeding joy. This is represented in three lively figures, as a shepherd's, an owner's, and a father's joy.

There is no doubt that we are intended to receive these as veritable and trustworthy illustrations of divine things. Whatever may be the philosophical value of that doctrine of the Incognoscibility of the Absolute, which, apparently a potent weapon of scepticism, Dr. Mansel strove so stoutly to wield in the service of orthodoxy, it is treason to all genuine heart religion to apply it to our conceptions of the attributes of God. Mr. Mill was indubitably right when he said that, "all trust in a revelation presupposes a conviction that God's attributes are the same in all but degree, with the best human attributes." If it be true, as Mansel seems to say, that we do not know what wisdom, justice, benevolence, mercy, are, as they exist in God, we can learn but little from Jesus, who always goes upon the assumption that we are made in the divine image, and draws his highest lessons in divinity from the common instincts of the human heart and the dictates of human conscience ; and who, especially and expressly on this high subject of a sinner's standing with his God, makes a direct appeal to universal feeling with his "What man is there of you who would not go in search of a lost sheep?" or "What woman would not sweep diligently to find a piece of silver?" and "A certain man had two sons."

This, in effect, is the argument of the first of these parables, "Is there a man of you who, if he had a hundred sheep, and one of them went astray, would not leave the ninety and nine, and go in search of the lost one ; and if he found it would not rejoice? And shall I not seek to save them that are lost, and rejoice when they are found? You sing, ' The Lord is my shepherd : ' ' we are his people, and the sheep of his pasture.' Is he not the shepherd of publicans ? And can he behold their wanderings without regret ? Is he to be a careless shepherd ? Must he not be glad when he finds a wanderer ? Yea, I say unto you, even as a shepherd beareth his lost sheep upon his shoulders, and calleth together his friends and neighbours, saying, Rejoice with me, for I have found my sheep which was lost ; likewise joy shall be in heaven over one sinner that repenteth."

If the second parable has less of sentimental attractiveness, it is even more profoundly suggestive. We need not trouble ourselves with the received opinion that its specialty is that it pays the honour due to the Third Person of the Trinity by illustrating his share in the work of salvation, the other parables being devoted respectively to the work of the Father and the Son. Those who find this in the parable shall for the present remain undisturbed in their belief, and in the enjoyment of the profound speculations on the significance of the candle, the coin, and the borom, which are to be found in the commentaries. For us the meaning of the parable here, as always, lies in the substance and drift of the story. It offers as its special contribution to the teaching of the chapter, a sharp and powerful exhibition of the idea of the value of a sinful soul. That idea, though present in the other parables, is subordinate—the object lost is a sentient creature with whose fate we sympathise, and in whose recovery we rejoice ; and we forget the seeker's personal interest—forget that it was on his own account that the shepherd called his neighbours to rejoice, that it was a pleasure and a joy to the father himself to see his ragged boy returning over the hill. But in the story of the woman and her piece of silver, as if to force upon us the great and difficult thought that our recovery is a matter of personal interest to the Most High, everything of a sentimental nature is eliminated, and we are invited to contemplate one who seeks purely for the value of the object lost, and rejoices with a purely personal joy. This is very bold teaching, so bold that we might have hesitated to use such an illustration, but being used by Jesus we receive it with reverent thankfulness, and try to believe the great truth it conveys—that the Almighty counts us as his, regards our fall as his loss, and desires us to believe that it is his interest that we should be restored. It is a customary expression of conventional piety, that he has no need of us or our praise or service to augment his infinite felicity and perfect glory; but it is also true and more conformable to the analogy of the faith, as we are taught here, that he has a personal property and interest in us, and seeks our salvation not only for our sake but in some sort also for his own.

In the concluding parable of the series, the divine joy is represented in that of a good father over a long-lost son. With the moving history of that son, and the conduct of his respectable but churlish brother, we have not now to do. We point—and only point to the picture of the father's joy. Here we can hardly speak of parable, for is not God in very deed our Father? It is the pure truth in concrete form. "And he arose, and came to his father. But when he was yet a great way off, his father saw him, and had compassion, and ran and fell on his neck, and kissed him. And the son said unto him, Father, I have sinned against heaven, and in thy sight, and am no more worthy to be called thy son. But the father said to his servants,

Bring forth the best robe, and put it on him ; and put a ring on his hand, and shoes on his feet : and bring hither the fatted calf, and kill it ; and let us eat, and be merry : for this my son was dead, and is alive again ; he was lost, and is found."

"Mercy and truth meet together ; righteousness and peace embrace each other."

"Thou desirest not sacrifice ; thou delightest not in burnt-offering. The sacrifices of God are a broken spirit : a broken and contrite heart thou wilt not despise."

"Let the wicked forsake his way, and the unrighteous man his thoughts : and let him return unto the Lord and he will have mercy upon him ; and to our God, for he will abundantly pardon. For my thoughts are not your thoughts, neither are your ways my ways, saith the Lord. For as the heavens are higher than the earth, so are my ways higher than your ways, and my thoughts than your thoughts."

"O God, who art long-suffering and kind, and art evermore seeking to turn us from our vanities, that we may live and not die ; Grant that we may know this the time of our visitation, and give ear to the voice that calleth us, and so bring us home, good Lord, from wandering in the wilderness, and give our weary hearts such rest in thee, that we may seek to wander from thee no more, but abide in thy peace for ever.   Amen."

XXVII.

THE NEW BIRTH.

THAT many should stumble at baptismal regeneration is not surprising, but there is no reason so apparent why so many, like Nicodemus, should marvel that Jesus says, " Ye must be born again."   In a former chapter it has been shown that the teaching of Jesus is always religious, always has reference to our relation to God, always pre-supposes a higher than the natural life ; and that though the form of the Synoptic discourses is different from that of the Johannine, there is no such difference of spirit as is sometimes alleged.   The difference of tone and phrase is apparent to the least critical student.   The writer of the Fourth Gospel, in which these words occur, dwells on certain aspects of the Master's teaching in a brooding fashion peculiar to himself, and in reporting his discourses he imparts to them the colour of his own meditative and somewhat mystical mind.

But there is really very little put into the Master's mouth for which a diligent reader of the other Gospels should not be prepared. No one who has understood the Sermon on the Mount can marvel that he should have said, " Ye must be born again."

While, however, we cordially accept this part of Christ's teaching, and indeed regard it as of fundamental value, we do so in no superstitious fashion. Persons of good and honest heart, who hear the word of Jesus and want to live as children of God and not of the devil, are not to suppose that they must await some supernatural visitation and be conscious of some extraordinary experience. " Turn ye unto me," saith the voice of ancient prophecy, " and I will pour out my spirit upon you." " Repent," says Jesus, " and ask the Holy Spirit, and he shall be given." No need, therefore, to look for some miraculous descent, when men trumpeting the marvels of a new revival, shall cry, " lo, here !" and " lo, there !" There were few stranger or sadder features of the recent American agitation in this country than its tendency to foster carnal notions regarding conversion and the work of the Spirit. Men spoke of his working in a fitful fashion, of his descending in a certain way at a certain hour, of anxious crowds waiting for his access. They seemed to fancy that he was at the beck of a few evangelists ; over the length and breadth of the land there spread a superstitious craving for their presence ; and one even read of piteous entreaties that if the great ones could not come themselves a satellite might be sent, if haply thus some stray rays of holy influence might be conveyed to them, and they should be converted and made whole. As if they had never heard the word of Jesus or been told of a way of life. As if God's good Spirit were not ever striving with them. As if anything were awanting but that they should forsake their sins and return to God.

The new birth in a man consists in an act of resolution on his part, an act done under a spiritual impulse and in faith of spiritual aids, but still an act of conscious resolution ; and the practical outcome of the text which has been made answerable for so much fanaticism is none other than this : " Repent, and believe the good news of God. Ask, and it shall be given you ; seek, and ye shall find. Your Father in heaven giveth the Holy Spirit to them that ask him."

We have in this reference to higher influences the note of religious, as distinguished from purely ethical, teaching. The popular love for Gospel sermons, though it may have degenerated into a piece of very sorry cant, rested on a true apprehension of the principles of the doctrine of Christ. A sermon may be truly and intensely Christian although Christian Pharisees shake their heads over it, and remark that Christ's name was never named ; although it does not contain a history of the fall, and an exposition of the doctrine of satisfaction ; although it is even as unevangelical as the Sermon on the Mount or the parables : but if it consists of mere useful advice and warning, never goes to the heart of the matter and opens the mystery of spiritual life, lets in no breath of heaven, no light of God, it is not a Christian sermon, because the truth of Christ is purely spiritual, comes from God, rests in God, leads to God ; not only giving a new commandment but inspiring a new obedience, and bringing a man under the powers of the world to come.

The question, therefore, whether a man has been converted or born again, though it has been so abused by the revivalistic school that it is in bad odour with many, is really a vital question. We may refuse to discuss it with every stranger who, puffed up with vain conceit, thrusts it upon us at first meeting, and thinks he is doing Christian work: but we may not omit to answer it to ourselves; for "we must be born again." It is doubtless painful to think how much despondency and misery many have had to undergo from mistaken views of conversion. Who can forget what even so robust and sincere a soul as Bunyan's had to endure in those two years and a half of wretched questioning and self-torture he has described so graphically? Who can remember the religious doubts that, seizing upon his constitutional malady, tormented the gentle spirit of Cowper to madness, and sent him to his grave in the gloom of despair, without some feeling of indignation against the bad theology which worked such mischief? For it is bad theology. If anxious souls are taught to look for the witness of their adoption in sudden flashes of conviction, in visions and revelations of the Lord, then is all manner of delusion encouraged, and those are made heavy whom God does not afflict. It is not so that the Spirit witnesseth with our spirits that we are the children of God, but by enabling us to call God our Father, and by working faith in us; by producing in us repentance, love, and new obedience, which, as they are the actual elements of Sonship, are the unmistakable tokens that we are born again. Approaching it in this way, the question of conversion is the question of life or death ; of love of sin or love of light ; of selfish worldliness or Christian self-denial : and thus apprehended, it is one which it is not safe for any man to leave untried. It is for the most part a sufficiently plain question as to which there can be little real difficulty. Any man can find out whether he is hungry for righteousness or greedy of gain ; whether he is pure in heart or full of vain desire ; whether he is trying to go in the narrow way or following the multitude in the broad ; whether he cares most for God's will or his own pleasure. These are issues which are by no means mysterious. We can judge in them and so can God : and if we will not, He assuredly will.

"Search me, O God, and know my heart : try me, and know my ways : and see if there be any wicked way in me, and lead me in the way everlasting."

XXVIII.

THE SALT OF THE EARTH.

THERE are two ways in which men influence one another, directly and indirectly. That we have the power of coercing or persuading others to act in a particular way we all know; we put forth effort for the purpose; and we have mostly some sense of the responsibility which is thereby entailed. We know also, but we do not sufficiently consider, that we exert an influence by the power of character and example which we cannot check or control, which is changed only by our character being changed, and which ceases not to operate when we have passed away. By this Abel, being dead, yet speaketh; by it we must speak in coming years for good or for ill.

It is of the latter powerful and pervasive influence that Jesus speaks when he says: "Ye are the light of the world. Ye are the salt of the earth." He speaks thus of the poor in spirit, the meek, the righteous, the lovers of peace; and it is a reason, additional to those that are of a personal kind, for cultivating the Christian graces, that it is thus the world is to be enlightened, thus that society is to be kept sweet and prevented from going to decay.

Men may be slow to believe when it is said in the simple language of the Old Testament that it is only for the sake of the righteous few that the Godless multitude is spared ; they may think that it belongs to a crude and obsolete way of conceiving the course of God's providence to represent the fate of Sodom and Gomorrha as depending upon the number of righteous persons that might be found within their walls : but no one will deny that by the time corruption has so far advanced in a community that ten moderately good men cannot be found, its doom is certain and cannot long be delayed. A nation will stand a great deal of bad government, and survive many disasters ; but one thing it must have, the salt of a sufficient number of honest men, or else it will decay. When these are few and their influence small, the most skilful diplomacy and the most dexterous strategy cannot eventually retard the inevitable ruin. Read the Bible and you will learn that "wheresoever the carcase is, there are the eagles gathered together." Read a very different book, Gibbon's *Decline and Fall of the Roman Empire*, and you will find the same lesson illustrated in the history of the nation which was the minister of final justice on the guilty city of God.

Christ calls upon his disciples to recognise their responsibility, and to give heed that directly and indirectly they promote the good of mankind. A selfish Christian is an absurdity : the spirit of Christ is that of active love and self-denying effort, and if any man have not this spirit, he is none of his. Christian influence is a living influence ; an influence not of mere doctrine or imposing machinery, but of living men on living men : it is inward and gradual, like that of leaven upon meal, by an unseen assimilation leavening the whole lump. Christian progress is most rapid and most sure when it is the result of the contagious enthusiasm of a few devoted men ; and while it has its ebb and flow, and is marked by crises like the day of Pentecost and the Reformation, it is like most great things, slow and quiet : " the Kingdom cometh not with observation." No better evangelistic method can be devised than that every member of the Christian Church should see that he lose not his own savour, that he have oil in his lamp and let his light purely shine.

There is no room to doubt that the great obstacle to the progress of Christianity in the world is the want of a simple strong faith among Christians, and the low level of the general Christian life. For our weakness in the faith, perhaps we are, in present circumstances, not altogether to blame; but for faults of conduct and sins against light we are always and entirely. Active missionaries at home and abroad, thoughtful observers of the signs of the times, alike Christian and heathen, agree in saying that the great obstacle to the conversion of the world is the insincerity of Christian profession and the inconsistency of Christian practice. Men are not sure that Christians believe their own creeds, and they plainly see that they do not obey Christ's precepts : and they say, 'If this is the fruit of your religion, we, judging by men's fruits, as Jesus himself directs, cannot greatly admire it.' Thoughtful youths at home, exposed to the temptations of their age, and distracted by the sceptical influences so rife at present, openly say that, comparing prominent types of Christianity with what they see among non-believing scientific men, or even honest gentlemen who make no profession, they had rather not be Christians. Educated Hindus whom we have taught enough to deprive them of their ancestral belief, and who occupy an attitude of inquiry towards Christianity, are staggered by what they see of British life in India. At home and in India there are many exceptions, brilliant and beautiful; but none the less is the general level low, and it is that which tells.

The want of the time is that Christians should live the life—every man, woman, and child of us. From this we are kept, mainly, of course, by our evil heart, but partly by subsidiary causes, two of which may be noted here. First, by undue reliance on machinery. An impression prevails that if we have our array of committees, managing each its little mission, and keeping up an edifying correspondence with its agents, and duly reporting to the "superior courts," all is well; that if funds are supplied to keep ministers from absolute starvation, and buy Bibles, and build churches and schools, the aggressive function of Christianity is sufficiently discharged; and that if, individually, the members of our congregations give their shillings or pence, and join in prayer for the spread of the Gospel, they have done their duty as lights of the world. Now, machinery is not to be despised, and organisation is admirable and indispensable. It is a poor thing to condemn salaried missionaries, and sneer at retiring allowances; "the labourer is worthy of his hire," and it is well, both for him and for the church that employs him, that his hire be regularly paid, and properly secured. But it is good to bear in mind the risk of becoming mechanical, and to acknowledge that, without a genuine Christian spirit, the best organisation cannot work well. When once more there is a real national faith; when we know a little better what to believe ourselves; when we live under the power of the simple but powerful law of Jesus; when there is amongst us a living church; then may some good work be hoped for in the world.

The other error is in an imperfect sense of individual responsibility. People delude themselves by talking of the church—as if it were some mysterious entity standing apart, and operating no one knows how; whereas it is simply the body of believers, whose life is their collective life, whose work is done by its several members in their place and station. They forget that, unless every one will do his part, the work cannot be properly done. This error is so common that the reference may be pardoned: it is so manifestly an error, that it would be unpardonable to dwell on it more.

XXIX.

THE TEST OF DISCIPLESHIP.

OUR Lord's own theory of the church is in the parable of the Vine. "I am the Vine ; ye are the branches. He that abideth in me, and I in him, the same bringeth forth much fruit : for without me, ye can do nothing." The church consists of those who receive his words and abide in his fellowship. His spirit is their life. They are known by the fruit they bear, that is, by their keeping of his commandments, and especially the new commandment he has given, that they should love one another. "By this shall all men know that ye are my disciples, that ye love one another."

Most of the rabbis had some peculiar tenet by their ostentatious adherence to which their followers were known. The schools of Hillel and Schammai were divided upon theoretical questions connected with the interpretation of the law ; and men knew their respective adherents by the colour of their opinions on those nice points. But Jesus had not tried to form a party on such lines. He had not lent himself at all to the legal quibbling which was in vogue. His grand object was to promote piety and good conduct among all classes, and particularly among the common people. His teaching, however, had its mark. As an expounder of religion and duty he is distinguished by his preaching of the law of love. As Newton brought light and order into natural science by establishing his great law, so Jesus, by a yet grander generalisation, showed that love is the ruling force in earth and in heaven. God is love; and love is the fulfilling of the law. But it is not by professing to receive this doctrine that his disciples are known. It is a faith which, if held sincerely, must bear fruit; and therefore, not fine talk about benevolence, but a life of charity and beneficence is the note of his church.

Other tests are arbitrary and delusive. It came to be maintained that the reception of sacraments is the badge of a Christian; that all baptized persons are Christians; and that none who have not undergone the rite are. This was long the ruling idea in Christendom; it has a certain power yet in certain quarters: but it need not be discussed here. It is openly at variance with our whole conception of the religion of Jesus to regard that as a certificate of true Christianity.

There are many who think that a disciple is to be known by his acceptance of the articles of one or another of the various creeds, in all their minute particulars. This, indeed, is the favourite modern test : and although it may seem not so irrational or flagrantly opposed to Christian principles as the former, it has not, in reality, any greater claim to be acknowledged. The creeds have greatly grown since Jesus was on the earth. They all profess to be drawn from the Scriptures ; but they differ greatly in their interpretations, and they have imported a good many philosophical assumptions and theories whose source is not to be found in Bible lands. They are records of battle. The articles bear marks of conflict, many of them, indeed, of internal conflict, having been fixed as they stand, after debate and division——that is to say, against the opinion of the minority, which may have included, and in fact, often did include, men as wise and as saintly as those whose sentiments prevailed.

When we consider that these idols of timid

and bigoted Christians are not infallible documents, but records of the opinions of the majority, in a certain church, at a particular date, it becomes conceivable that men may be worthy Christians, although they incline rather to the opinion of the minority, which, once within a few votes of being "the truth," perhaps is now called heresy. And if the documents have not been revised for two or three hundred years,—inasmuch as the world has not been standing still all that time, but been making astonishing progress in the knowledge of many things which have important bearing upon ecclesiastical doctrine,—it is even conceivable that a man may be a very good Christian, though he finds them both erroneous and defective. And of this there is no doubt, that a man may believe, or at any rate, say that he believes, every jot and tittle of them, without having the faintest spark of Christian spirit, or showing the least sign of Christian fruit.

Still less to be commended are those party tests, which are so much in favour with those of the straiter sect of our religion; which are not only fallacious, but mischievous and detestable. When the followers of Christ get split up into sections and coteries, and party spirit runs high, and men say, "I am of Paul, and I of Apollos, and I of Cephas," or, worst of all, "I am of Christ;" when they refuse to recognise as brethren any who cannot pronounce their shibboleths, and walk in all their ways; when none but evangelicals here, none but High Church there, and none but revivalists elsewhere, are allowed to be "truly good," "genuine Christians," then we have confusion and every evil work.

The Master's own test is the true one, the infallible one. It is the one which eventually the world is sure to apply. When they see us obeying this law, they will be more ready to glorify our Father which is in Heaven. Time was when the heathen said, "Behold how they love one another!" One of the ablest and keenest enemies Christianity has encountered bore testimony to their practice in this reproach addressed to his heathen subjects: "It is a shame when the Jews suffer none of theirs to beg, and even the impure Galileans relieve not only their own, but also those of our religion, that we only should fail in so necessary a duty." Let any honest Christian say whether, by any stretch of charity, or any figment of self-esteem, it can be said of the church as it now is in the earth, that it corresponds in any adequate degree to its founder's idea, or to the pattern left by his apostles and friends. Are mutual good-will and kindly co-operation the distinguishing marks of those who bear the Christian name? Is this what men recognise unfailingly in the church—a society of persons bound together in a brotherhood of common loyalty to a heavenly Lord and mutual love among themselves? Is this the thing which, above all others, as church-members we see each in the other—the spirit of the one Lord calling us to love and good works? For my part, I know no church, not even my own, which I love best, and whose faults I do not willingly see, that has held up in sufficient prominence, and worked out with proper persistency, this first principle of a true Christianity. We have wandered in many ways from the primitive simplicity and purity, but we have in no respect more grievously fallen behind than in this ; and the sooner we set about the task of giving this doctrine its rightful place in our preaching, and endeavouring to regulate our personal and social life accordingly, the better will it be for the church and for the world. No baptismal privilege, no frequency of communion, no orthodoxy of opinion, no reputation of sentimental piety will, in the face of defect and transgression in this the true fundamental, persuade men to believe we are the disciples of Jesus; still less induce him, who cannot be deceived and will not be mocked, to confess us before the Father which is in Heaven.

XXX.

UNITY.

JESUS himself nowhere speaks of the Church.
That is a word of later origin ; but it undoubtedly represents an idea whose foundations lie deep and sure in his teaching. His
view of life is distinctively social. His purpose
was to gather his people into a brotherhood,
a society animated by his spirit, a society having a real corporate life of its own. St. Paul
worthily speaks of it as the body of Christ.
He himself expounded his idea of it, under the
similitude of the Vine and the branches ; and
the phrase of his which most nearly designates
it is the " household of God," or the " kingdom
of heaven."

From what has been said concerning this
it follows, as indeed at this stage it should be
unnecessary to say, that all questions of form,
ministry, and government are secondary. To
make them primary, to insist on the divine

right of any particular form of church government or the necessity of an outward and material transmission of divine gifts, or the saving efficacy of sacraments, seems not only to be unwarranted by anything in the recorded sayings of Jesus, but to be evidently opposed to the substance and meaning of his doctrines. As long as you keep to purely spiritual conceptions, no doctrine about the church can be too high; but when you come to deal with rites and ceremonies of human invention, and bearing on them very plainly the marks of their origin, no doctrine can be too low.

While the highest importance is to be attached to unity of spirit, we need not be greatly concerned about outward uniformity. We can readily believe that Jesus prayed concerning his disciples, "that they all may be one, as thou, Father, art in me, and I in thee;" and also, that he must have desired to see his followers held together in the unity of the Spirit, in the bond of that love in which he and the Father are one. Beyond all question, the existence and manifestation of this unity would have had the effect of inducing the world to believe that the Father had sent him. In this unity, therefore, in the communion of saints,

in the holy church universal, we believe : but
for unity of opinion, or taste, or custom ; for
uniformity of creed, and worship, and church
organisation, except in so far as these may
help the true unity, we do not greatly care.

Unity of spirit is a note, or if you will, the
note of the church. No language of the highest of High Churchmen is strong enough to
express the value, the supreme indispensableness
of this quality. But when such language is
employed with reference to a particular ecclesiastical system, and we are told that unless where
there are bishops duly ordained in apostolic
succession, and sacraments administered by men
in regular orders, the Spirit of the Lord cannot be found, and the blessing of salvation is
withheld, and there is no church at all,—it sounds
to some of us not only ridiculously strong, but
altogether false and well-nigh blasphemous.
To say that substantial unity and genuine
brotherhood cannot subsist without this uniformity, seems a very strange and unworthy
thing, which is not warranted by fact or reason.
Unity of spirit does exist where uniformity is
not only neglected but scouted and contemned :
and does not always exist where it is found and
cherished. On this latter point, at all events,

there can be no doubt, for outward uniformity has been sufficiently tried. It has been, indeed, hitherto the leading principle of the church; for fifteen centuries it was applied exclusively, with every advantage, and with undeniable vigour and skill; and the history and present condition of Christendom may show how far the endeavour to have one fold as well as one flock has tended to the increase of peace on earth and good-will among men.

But would it not be desirable that there should be in the earth one grand compact Christian church? It is by no means certain that it would. In matters of creed, worship, and government, the opinions and tastes of men are so various that the unity of Christendom is more likely to be promoted by separate societies than by one. The religion of different nations will flourish best in national churches, and even within a nation many men have many minds. History bears bloody witness to the criminal folly of seeking to impose upon an unwilling people an uncongenial form; and absolute agreement of opinion, were it desirable, is not to be attained. It is not necessary to admire or defend existing divisions; it is quite open to us to confess that the present state of matters

in Scotland is a scandal and a farce: but nevertheless, it may not be unreasonable to doubt
as to the practicability of current theories of
union, and to take but slender interest in the
various schemes whose noise now fills the air.

There are two methods chiefly in vogue for
healing our divisions. There is the method of
absorption, the High Church method advocated
in Scotland with so much power and fervour by
Bishop Wordsworth in the ears of a people,
stiff-necked enough in most things, but especially so in this of prelacy. No one who has
read Dr. Wordsworth's appeals, certainly no one
who has heard them, can fail to esteem his learning and piety ; but while we entertain for himself a respectful and almost affectionate admiration, it is impossible to help regretting the
waste of so much fine talent and earnestness,
and looking upon him and his Anglican friends
as men who are beating the air, and chasing a
shadow with infinite pains. No : if we cannot
be saved without a threefold ministry and
authentic sacraments, we will rather have them
undoubtedly genuine, and follow Drs. Manning
and Newman all the way.

The other method is that of coalition, the
plan most in favour in churches on the Presby-

terian model. It has been tried with some success abroad ; hitherto, with something considerably short of success, at home. One can only rejoice to hear that in the large air of Canada and Australia, our fellow-countrymen have come to see the folly of pepetuating the narrow political squabbles which are the subject of our national schisms ; but there is not much in the history of the ten years' abortive conflict about union between the Free and United Presbyterian Churches, or in the present temper and attitude of either towards the Established Church, to induce one to look for much in the way of unity, as the fruit of ecclesiastical politics and dexterous negotiation.

Better far is the method of Jesus, which is that of oneness of spirit. Not till this prevails, and men have learnt to think more of Christ himself than of this or that view of his headship ; more of prayer than of the question whether the minister shall read or recite, and the people stand or kneel ; more of God's glory than of the sinfulness of listening to an organ ; more, in fine, of the weightier matters of the law, than of such things of an outward and temporary kind as now engross so much attention ; not till this comes to pass—and the signs of it are not many at the present hour—is there much hope of such an union of Scottish Christians, as I should think worthy of our efforts and prayers.

It remains to say what, perhaps, will meet with less sympathy, but is even more obviously true, that, while unity of faith is essential to the life of the church, this is by no means the case with uniformity of belief or doctrine, to which is attached an importance so exaggerated. Men will never think alike on such matters as are embraced in our theologies. Though we should all resolve to hold the same opinions on some disputed point of theology or politics, or taste, or manners, we could not do it : we might agree to use the same words, but we could not force ourselves to think the same thoughts. As long as there are many men there will be many minds. The opinions of men are moulded by their idiosyncrasies, their education, their environment ; and we have already sought to distinguish between opinion which is various, and faith which is one. Peter and Paul, James and John served the same Lord and preached the same Gospel, but on some points, and these of no slight importance, they propounded views as various as those of men of one spirit could well be. There is no harm in such difference. The harm is when men lose their temper in discussion, and make mountains of molehills, and grow hard and uncharitable, and excommunicate, and give ill names ; for that breaks the unity of spirit, and snaps the sacred bond of peace.

Readers of the *Life of Sterling* will remember how it is told that, when he and Carlyle became acquainted, they walked westward by lanes and quietest streets, " talking on moralities, theological philosophies ; arguing copiously, but, *except in opinion, not disagreeing.*" When shall we disciples of Jesus learn this most Christian lesson, and preserve agreement of temper and affection, unity of spirit, though we differ ever so widely in what we call doctrine, which is, to so large extent, matter not of faith, but only of opinion ?

XXXI.

MISSIONS.

IT was part of the work of Jesus, to which he gave special attention, to train his disciples to be teachers themselves, that his gospel might be carried to all nations; and it is an unfailing characteristic of those who truly receive his words, that they are eager to communicate to others the truth which has made them free.

There is something very fine in the close of St. Matthew's Gospel. "Go ye, therefore, and make disciples of all nations, baptizing them in the name of the Father, and of the Son, and of the Holy Ghost; teaching them to observe all things, whatsoever I have commanded you : and lo, I am with you alway, even unto the end of the world." Critics may doubt whether the Lord actually uttered them as they stand; but it is impossible to deny that they fitly embody the splendid audacity of apostolic enterprise,

R

and that they have been abundantly justified by the event. They express the strong faith in the truth of the Gospel, and the power of their Master's spirit, which made a few obscure men calmly undertake the spiritual conquest of the world. "All things are possible to him that believeth."

The point that has to be noted here is that Christianity is, from its very nature, aggressive, and that it is not on apostles and missionaries alone, but on every disciple, that the duty is laid of spreading the good news. Never was a greater perversion of any system than that which would turn the religion of Jesus into a scheme of spiritual selfishness, and allow its votaries to think that it consisted merely in saving their own souls. Selfishness is not the less selfishness that it clothes itself in a garb of piety; perhaps that which has not inaptly been called other-worldliness is a more unlovely thing than downright worldliness of the common kind; and at all events a selfish Christian, a Christian who has no care for others, comes as near as may be to a contradiction in terms.

What, then, is to be said of Protestantism in its aggressive capacity? Have the churches of the Reformation done their part as missionary societies ? Has their success been such as might reasonably have been expected ?

To answer the last question first, it must be said that it has not. Protestantism has, in this important respect, hitherto failed. The statement may be unwelcome, but it must be made. When we remember the spread of the gospel in the early centuries, the career of the great missionaries of the Middle Ages, the conquests of the Roman Church—the aggregate results of Protestant missionary enterprise do not seem to be much to boast of. When we reflect that the reformed churches are, or consider themselves to be, the most enlightened of all, that they enjoy the favour of the most powerful nations, and the enormous advantages offered by modern discovery and invention, the spread of commerce, the ease of travel and communication ; above all, when we think of the magnificent promises of the Scriptures, and the aspirations of devout souls who believe that in this work men are in a special sense fellow-workers with God—it is impossible to resist the conclusion that Protestant missions have been a failure on the whole.

Among the causes of this must be mentioned the fact, far from creditable to Protestant churches, that for a long time little was attempted in the way of missions. An excuse for this at first might be found in the struggling and persecuted condition of the reformed communities; but this apology is not available for the churches of Britain in the eighteenth century, during which the history of missions is nearly a blank. It was reserved for the present century to witness a genuine outbreak of the missionary spirit. If this be borne in mind, and if it be considered how few even yet in our congregations really care whether the heathen are saved or not, the small result hitherto achieved need excite no surprise.

It must be remembered, also, that heroic efforts have often been misdirected. It has been alleged that the friends of missions have shown a strange preference for the unhealthiest spots on the face of the globe; and though that is hardly just, it is not to be denied that there are passages in the history of early missions to the coast of Africa which give some ground for the reproach. There is something to admire in the zeal and constancy of the promoters of such enterprises, and very admirable indeed is the devotion of the successive bands who volunteered as for a forlorn hope; but it is sad to think how many countries there were in the wide world where the preachers might have had a chance of surviving, and would have found multitudes as much in need of help, and more capable of civilisation.

A like reflection is suggested by the records of missions to inferior and decaying races. There is no finer figure in Christian history than that of Eliot, the apostle of the North American Indians, no more touching story than that of his life; but the redskin has vanished from the plains where he laboured, and of his noble work no result remains but the little library of grammars and Bibles in those barbarous dialects, interesting to philologists as a monument of an extinct form of human speech, but of no other use any more in the world. Is there not room to fear that the same may yet be true of the islands of the Pacific? There is not in all the catalogue the name of a greater saint than John Coleridge Pattison, the record of whose Christlike life and martyr-death is among the choicest treasures of the universal church; but it is saddening to think that this, too, may be another instance of labour and sacrifice thrown away. Not that either Eliot's or Pattison's work has been in vain; but it might have yielded far greater results if it had been bestowed upon races which had some promise of permanence, some capacity of improvement, some prospect of playing a part in the future history of mankind.

Another thing which cannot fail to be a source of weakness and failure is the want of union and co-operation among Protestant Christians. Division is weakness; and when to division are added confusion and strife, we cannot hope to command, and do not deserve, success. It is bad enough when sects at home compete for recruits instead of fishing for souls; when their agents jostle each other in the lanes of London or the wynds of Glasgow: but in the foreign field we should shun the appearance of such rivalry,—seeking rather the strength of union, and the comfort of brotherly co-operation, which would not only tend to the benefit of the heathen, but be full of blessed results for ourselves.

The influence of our ancient creeds and intricate theologies, if we would confess it, must be a hindrance to success. Those confessions and catechisms to which our timid and faithless Christianity clings with such passionate conservatism, having in the first instance widely departed from the simplicity of Jesus, are a little antiquated and are very fast becoming obsolete at home. The earthen vessel in which our divine treasure is contained waxeth old and is ready to decay. Besides, were this as doubtful as it is obvious, there is no room to doubt that systems so metaphysical and minute are unsuitable for missionary purposes. Nothing can be better adapted for universal use than the words of Jesus, so simple and so full of spiritual power, but it is different with Protestant theology which bears so deeply the impress of western culture and European polemics. Those who think it wise, may continue to teach their own infants about the creation of the world in the space of six days, and the decrees of God and effectual calling ; but they may without offence be invited to consider whether the Shorter Catechism is the best manual for the training of simple Africans or subtle Hindoos. By all means let our missionaries be the ablest men we can find, disciplined in all critical learning, and informed with the results of our highest culture ; but when they meet the heathen let them leave their catechisms and confessions behind, and say nothing about theories of inspiration and predestinarian dogmas. Let them make their New Testament their manual of divinity, and even in it prefer the parables of Jesus to the disquisitions of Paul ; and let them leave the new converts to develop for themselves such forms as they may require, of native make and native fashion.

But alas ! we have first to learn a great deal at home ; and this perhaps is the ultimate truth on this subject at present, that we are too unsettled, too anxious, too critical, to be great missionaries.   We are in the throes of a revolution, though many of us know it not, and we must gain some clearness and stability for ourselves, before we can teach others.   When we or our children have attained a simple and lively faith, and religion is once more a real power in our own land, then we shall set about the task of enlightening the dark places of the earth with more vigour and more hopefulness, and, please God, with more success.

XXXII.

BAPTISM.

THE twelve were to go and make disciples of all nations, baptizing them in the name of the Father, and of the Son, and of the Holy Ghost, teaching them to observe all things whatsoever the Lord had commanded. Baptism first, instruction afterwards. This is the natural order. Baptism is the initiatory rite, the sign of one's receiving the good news, and being willing to become a disciple of Jesus; of his consenting to learn what Jesus has to teach, and to obey what he commands. In the case of adults this implies a certain amount of preliminary instruction; but as soon as the main facts and principles of Christianity were known and accepted, as soon as a man had resolved to forsake his idols and turn to God, it was meet that the sign of admission to the new covenant should be administered : it could of itself do nothing for him, but his faith in Christ had already changed his position, and it was right that that change should be signified in the generally understood way.

The practice of infant baptism is perfectly justifiable, although we do not regard it as having itself a regenerating power. We do not baptize children because we think that if we do they are safe, if we do not they will be damned. We cannot believe that the eternal destiny of any child of God hangs on a thread so slender, or that the things of the Spirit are so dependent on material means. And when our friends of the so-called Baptist persuasion ask us why then we administer the rite to unconscious infants, in whom the spiritual life has not begun, and who cannot understand anything of the name in which they are baptized, or of the duties and privileges of discipleship, why we do not wait till the child can embrace Christ as offered in the gospel, and we can have some confidence that our rite corresponds to and describes a real fact,—we answer that we use it as a sign of something out of ourselves altogether, which depends not on us but on God, as a certificate, not of present or prospective holiness, but of God's mercy and Fatherly love. It is a fact which we believe as Christian people, that our children are in the spiritual sense children of God, heirs of that kingdom which is righteousness and peace and joy in the Holy Ghost; and it is this faith we testify when we bring them to be baptized, avowing, at the same time, our purpose to teach them in due time to observe all things which the Lord hath commanded. Instead of proceeding to instruct a child in Christian truth on the footing that it is an open question whether he shall be a Christian or not, we are encouraged to treat him from the first as a redeemed creature in the purpose of God, to appeal to his baptism as a sign of an heavenly calling, to exhort him and instruct him to walk worthy of it always. This is the order of Scripture, and is according to the analogy of the faith which represents the divine life as planted in God's Fatherliness, rooted and grounded in his love, bringing forth the blossoms of a glad and trustful piety, and the blessed fruit of righteous deeds.

This is all that is to be said concerning baptism here, the monstrous growth of later superstition and controversy having its ground elsewhere than in the teaching of Jesus of Nazareth.

XXXIII.

THE LORD'S SUPPER.

THE supper also is a stronghold of superstition
and a subject of controversy ; and it differs
from baptism in this, that the sacramentarian
theory professes to be founded on the express
words of Jesus. It happens that the account
of the Last Supper is the clearest and best
authenticated of all the traditions, and may
rank as unquestionably historical. It might
stand as a simple enough story of a very touching incident and a sufficient warrant for a
venerable rite, but for the fact that, in taking a
piece of bread and giving it to his disciples,
Jesus said, " Take, eat, this is my body ;" and
that on these words is founded the Popish dogma
of transubstantiation, the central position of the
only sacramentarian system which requires serious consideration. The bread is changed into
the body of Christ by or during the service
performed by the officiating priest, who offers it

to God as a real sacrifice ; and the faithful, eating the consecrated wafer, do then verily eat the flesh of the Son of man, and lay hold on everlasting life.

Against this it is of no avail to allege that the bread remains bread, as it was before ; because you are met by the assertion, that it does so remain in respect of all outward and perceptible qualities, but that nevertheless its substance is changed into that of the Lord's blessed body——a proposition against which reasonable argument is vain.

But inasmuch as it is alleged that the church was driven to assert this most extraordinary of miracles, by the exigency of being faithful to the plain words of Scripture, it is necessary to say that the literal interpretation put upon those words is not only a wrong one, palpably false, but is, moreover, far-fetched and unnatural. This requires to be said with some emphasis, because the strength of the contrary opinion is historically vouched by the example of Luther and the invention of the dogma of consubstantiation, and even among ourselves an impression prevails that there is much to be said for the Romish view, and that our Protestant explanation is but an ingenious make-shift, which does not solve, but evades the difficulty.

As has been already, more than once, observed, the literal is not always the true sense, especially in the case of the words of Jesus. When one recals his most familiar sayings, it seems nothing short of an absurdity to say that when he took up a bit of bread, and said, " This is my body," he could have no other meaning than that which the words literally convey. Is it reasonable to suppose, that the apostles could have any doubt as to his meaning, or that the idea of a transubstantiation could ever have entered their minds ?   And, if we must read "This is my body " literally, what are we to make of these words, " This cup is the new testament in my blood ?"

The truth is, that, far from being natural and obvious, the literal interpretation is, in this case, so far-fetched, that it is a marvel that it should ever have been suggested, and have acquired such a hold upon men with Bibles in their hands.

It is of more importance to remark that the 'corporal and carnal' view of this ordinance is opposed to the analogy of the Christian faith. It is hard to understand how any disciple of

Jesus should attach such weight to matters of an external kind ; how, even supposing the dogma of transubstantiation to be credible, it should be believed that the physical eating of the body of Jesus could produce any spiritual result. If it were not a gigantic, and now very ancient fact, one would have been ready to use the well-known language of Cicero, regarding a scarcely more foolish error of a similar kind : "That no man could be so mad as to believe such things." Feeling, indeed, that all this, largely as it has occupied and still occupies the thoughts of Christians, is quite away from the subject of this book, and opposed to the truth which it sets forth, I enter no further into the subject, and offer an apology for making even this short chapter so long.

XXXIV.

THE TARES.

ON the subject of evil, so full of dark questions as old as the dawn of thought, so puzzling and so painful to meditative minds, Jesus says generally, "Let not your heart be troubled; believe in God, believe also in me," and embodies some wise, practical counsel, in the parable of the Tares in the Field.

He offers no final philosophical solution of the problem of the Origin of Evil. In some of the Old Testament Scriptures, in the Book of Ecclesiastes, in certain of the Psalms, and chiefly in the marvellous poem of Job, it is, in several aspects, grappled with, but it cannot be said to have been solved. Nor is it solved by Jesus. The Master, indeed, in the parable, in reply to his servants' query, "Whence came the tares?" says, "An enemy hath done this," but the question still arises, Why was an enemy allowed to do this? why is an enemy of the Almighty suffered to exist at all? For anything which we can adduce from the teaching of the Lord this old puzzle must be left in its original darkness. He has not added one to the many solutions which have been offered, and his disciples will most wisely take the implied hint and leave it alone. "Before a confessed and unconquerable difficulty," Stanley writes of Arnold, "his mind reposed as quietly as in possession of a discovered truth." If to this wise repose in presence of speculative difficulty we add that resolute girding up of one's-self to do battle with evil in its practical forms, of which we have no better example than that furnished by Arnold's life, we shall do well. When they said to him, "Lord, are there few that be saved?" Jesus answered and said, "Strive to enter in at the strait gate." "The secret things," it is written in the old law, "belong unto the Lord our God, but those things which are revealed belong unto us and to our children for ever, that we may do all the words of this law."

Not then as a philosophical solution, but as a practical counsel, is this parable to be judged; and as such, it has a high value. To the devout soul, vexed by the conversation of ungodly men, and saddened by the abounding misery of life, to whom not as an intellectual puzzle but as an agonising doubt and fear there comes the question, Can such things be, if God is as the Lord would have us believe? Jesus says, "An enemy hath done this;" you must believe this, and abide the end. Believe that an enemy of God is the author of evil, not God; let nothing tempt you to ascribe what is evil to him in any shape or form. Whatever logic may seem to require, whatever doubt may suggest, be careful to keep your idea of him clear from any association, or appearance of connivance, with evil. Believe that he is its irreconcilable and relentless foe; believe that he is on the side of those who fight against it, and that his cause, the cause of light, must prevail.

On the practical question concerning the purity of the church, this parable gives a lesson much, but not wisely, neglected. Students of ecclesiastical history know how, in the fourth century, a fierce controversy arose regarding this matter, which rent the church and threatened the peace of the world. And ever and anon there springs up some sect, often very small, which aims at making the visible church as pure as that ideal spouse of whom so glorious things are spoken. Indeed, as Archbishop Trench has remarked, "every young Christian, in the time of his first zeal, is tempted to be somewhat of a Donatist in spirit ; nay, it would argue little love or holy earnestness in him if he had not this longing to see the church of his Saviour a glorious church, without spot or wrinkle." But the Lord himself says, " Let both grow together ;" do not anticipate the judgment of God, lest by your hasty zeal you do more harm than good ; rest assured that God is wise, and that his wisdom will be justified in due time.

Not that the mixture of good and evil in the church or the world is a matter of indifference to God or to men. That he seems not to care has been the great trial of good men—thinking, in their haste, that, if they had his power they would make short work with many things that he tolerates or spares. Zealous men chafe at his long-suffering, and are offended by his patience. But Jesus bids us remember that he knows it all, and is wiser than we ; bids us leave the issue in his hand, secure that he watcheth over his field, and that no enemy shall be suffered, eventually, to spoil the fruit and increase of his blessed word. God is not indifferent to the tares, and we need not, and should not, be. Tares are tares, though they may for a while be suffered to grow, and the end of them is to be burned ; and though sincere Christians are encouraged not to be troubled because false Christians abound, it is impossible not to regret the harm they do to the good cause, by giving occasion to the enemy to blaspheme, and by putting a stumbling-block in the way of youthful friends.

Nor is this to damp the ardour of Christian effort, or excuse a lukewarm temper. This parable cannot be wrested into an argument for the easy-minded policy of " let alone." If it be said, What is the use of disquieting ourselves about the state of the world, and labouring for the regeneration of society ?—are we not told, that there will be good and evil together until the end? Nay, are we not expressly commanded to let both grow together till the harvest ? It must be replied, first of all, we are not told to let both grow together ; it is the reapers that receive this charge, and the reapers are the angels : secondly, there will be good and evil, wheat and tares, but woe to them who are found among the tares ; woe also to them who do not seek to do good as they have opportunity.

We are not to execute hasty judgment; but we are straitly required to " bear one another's burdens, and so fulfil the law of Christ."

The lesson for us from this parable is that, while the true church is pure and spotless, the actual church, in its outward form and historical manifestation, must partake of human imperfection; and that attempts to make the visible church co-extensive and identical with the invisible are unwise. If all other reasons in support of this prudent counsel should fail, this ought to suffice, that the endeavour is one in which success is impossible. We can certainly expel notorious offenders, and exercise a wise and godly discipline; but when attempts have been made to strain the power of discipline, they have always broken down and commonly led to more ungodliness. And we cannot deal with secret offenders, or bring into judgment those sins of the temper and of the heart which are the most deadly of all. We may by such endeavours give an extraordinary encouragement to hypocrisy, which little needs any encouragement, and which is, in the sight of the Lord, the sorest evil under the sun. We should seriously discourage many weak brethren, and trouble humble and anxious souls. And we should offer an inlet to uncharitableness and censoriousness, to secret spying and tale-bearing, the very imagination of which is sufficient to appal.

"Judge not, that ye be not judged." "Vengeance is mine; I will repay, saith the Lord."

XXXV.

THE BOX OF OINTMENT.

"All subtle thought, all curious fears
  Borne down by gladness so complete,
  She bows, she bathes the Saviour's feet
With costly spikenard and with tears."

THE disciples, following the lead of Judas, objected to the waste; the Master not only defended Mary's action, but gave it emphatic praise. In the complaint of the disciples, leaving Judas out of account, we have the judgment of coolness upon warm enthusiasm, of matter of fact upon sentiment. The act of Mary was an act of enthusiastic affection, an expression of feelings peculiarly tender and intense with which they, albeit they loved the Master in their own way, could not sympathise. He appreciated it, and stood between her and her critics ; he would not have her sensitive feelings wounded, and first of all, he said sharply, " Let her alone."

A warning against narrow-minded, and, which

is worse, narrow-hearted, criticism of our neighbour; a lesson that we should make allowance for difference of temper, and remember that a thing is not necessarily wrong because it is not exactly in our way. A warning in particular to persons of cool temperament and inclined to sobriety not to judge too hastily their more impulsive and demonstrative neighbours; not to conclude that all who are, as they think, a little extravagant in their piety must be hypocritical or mischievous. If zeal may be made a cloak of maliciousness, moderation is often alleged as an excuse for apathy and laziness. " Let every man be fully persuaded in his own mind," and let no man go out of his way to find fault with others who prefer a more elaborate worship, a more emotional piety, lest haply he trouble some tender hearts whose devotion is pleasant in the sight of the Lord.

It must be allowed that the objectors in this instance alleged a plausible reason. " It might have been sold for three hundred pence, and given to the poor." It seemed a large sum to spend in compliment; it did the Lord no positive good; had it been judiciously expended in procuring substantial comforts, many a poor family would have been made glad. That looks like a strong argument, and one which a friend of the poor and teacher of self-denial was bound to approve. But no; he praised Mary: "She hath done a good work on me. The poor ye have with you always, but me ye have not always" (the shadow of coming death was on him). "She hath done what she could."

It need not be said that Jesus is no friend of sinful waste, or of neglect of the poor; but it is important to notice how, with that large wisdom which is so remarkable, he recognises that unnecessary expenditure is not always waste, and that there are other ways of doing good than by giving money to the poor. This is a valuable safeguard against attempts, whether made by foes or by friends, to identify Christianity with a hard and niggardly asceticism, and to draw from its principles arguments against all expenditure which is directed to luxury in life and beauty in worship. There are some who, in private life, doubt whether it is right to spend money on the amenities; some who, in public affairs, grumble if national revenues are devoted to any other purpose than those of actual administration and defence, and ask, What is the use of grants for picture galleries, and expeditions to the North Pole? And there are good men who, in matters connected with religion, object to the laying out of more money on the fabric of churches or the external aids of worship than is absolutely necessary, and denounce all beauty of architecture and music as sinful extravagance. 'Spend money on your own luxuries or in paying compliments to your friends, when there are poor creatures in the world who know not where to find a dinner! Let government, if it has money to spare, give it to our swarming poor, or build asylums, and not squander it on empty shows and sentimental enterprises. Let Christians, if they have so much to devote to God's service, expend it in works of charity, and not in needless ornament. Your church has cost so many hundreds or thousands of pounds more than a perfectly plain one would have done: why was not all this saved to build another church, or given to the poor?'

Perhaps it may be observed that this kind of argument is often heard from people who are well known to have prejudices of their own against fine churches or organs on quite other grounds; and that it may not be certain, any more than it was in the case of Judas, that the objection is absolutely sincere.

It might also be remarked with profit that it takes far more wisdom and far more trouble than most people think to help the poor; that it certainly is not a good plan to hand over to them the savings of the industrious, and the surplus of the rich; and that whatever advantages might result from restricting expenditure to the limits of a bare necessity, and giving the balance to the poor, this course would not relieve but intensify pauperism.

It would also be fair to require from those who argue for the barely necessary in matters ecclesiastical, that they should carry out their principles consistently. If they act in this way in personal and domestic arrangements, they have at least a right to be heard when they protest against costly churches and fine music; but if they do not disdain such comforts and luxuries as they can command, we must be excused if we find them slightly inconsistent, and call upon them to apply their principles in other spheres than that of religion. As long as we are agreed that money spent upon art is not necessarily thrown away, and that there are worse ways of using it than in satisfying a cultivated love of beautiful sights and sounds, so long must we maintain that expenditure on cathedrals and organs may be not only capable of defence, but worthy of praise. There is something admirable in the old desire to glorify God by rearing stately churches which should tower in solemn grandeur above the other buildings of the city, and filling them with costly marbles and artistic carvings, and "storied windows richly dight." There is something also in the feeling which made David unwilling to dwell in a house of cedar while the ark remained under curtains, and prompted Solomon to lavish the resources of his kingdom on a magnificent temple whose description occupies a large space in Holy Writ. It is nothing less than a shame, indeed, for people who know what is good in architecture, and can afford to build palaces for themselves, to worship in squalid churches ; for those who love music, and cultivate it in private, to be content with bad singing in the house of God. I have known a church, as plain and ugly as might be, wherein there ministered a man of fine taste, whose whole service was full of regard for the beauty of holiness, and I could not help wishing that his surroundings had been more in harmony with his style : and when I looked round and saw in the congregation several men who had a great deal more money than they knew what to do with—men whose houses were furnished and decorated with costly elegance—I could not but think there was something wrong when they were willing to worship God in such a place, and that some degree of extravagance and apparent waste would have been better, certainly better for themselves, than such withholding. The poor need not have suffered, and would not have suffered. These things they should have done, and not have left the other undone.

XXXVI.

NOT PEACE, BUT A SWORD.

ANOTHER example of the sanctified wisdom of
Jesus is furnished by his forecast of the future.
Confident of the final triumph of his doctrine,
he saw that its progress would not be smooth,
nor its success sudden ; that the gospel of peace
would be a source of strife and division. "I
am not come to send peace on earth, but a
sword." As in a diseased body healing must
often involve increased suffering for a time, and
can only be purchased by pain, so must a sick
world suffer before the rooted evils of ages can
be cured ; as peace in the soul is the reward of
victory in the good fight of faith, so must there
be conflict in the world before truth and right
prevail. Old iniquities die hard, and men will
fight for their idols, and quarrel about their
opinions ; there will be opposition and persecution, schisms and cruelties, assaults from the
infidel and crusades against him, persecutions of

heretics and religious wars. That peace might triumph, the sword must prevail for a time.

"For I am come to set a man at variance against his father, and the daughter against her mother, and the daughter-in-law against her mother-in-law, and a man's foes shall be they of his own household." Knowing that all men would not believe, he saw that division must arise—not difference merely, but strife, estrangement, and hostility. Because of ignorance and stupidity, because of the tenacity with which men cling to their own opinions and the customs they have learned, because of evil tempers and passions, there would be division even in families where the new light should shine. It could not otherwise be. Setting aside wickedness or Pharisaism—two powerful factors of mischief— and making allowance for the natural unwillingness of an orthodox Jew to receive strange doctrines and have himself expelled from the synagogue, we see how discord must have arisen. The religion which he preferred, and which, as it seemed, Jesus wished to destroy, had on its side the awful sanctities of Sinai and the venerable prescription of fifteen hundred years. He had learned it from his mother, and it had been commended to him with his father's dying breath. He was a member, we will say, of the priestly caste, and by long use the ceremonies of the temple had become dear. Could such a man be expected to allow his son or daughter to follow Jesus without some feeling of indignation and regret ? Just because he was a sincere man, and regarded religion as the chief thing, he must be grieved and angry; he would try to persuade his son to abjure the pestilent heresy, and bring him back to the venerable faith of Israel ; if he should fail, there remained a wall of separation, and the more deeply they felt on the subject the more serious would the division be. It was a pity, but there was, indeed, nothing left in such a case but for a man to leave his father and his mother, and take up the cross and follow Jesus.

If for such a conservative Jew we substitute a sincere Roman Catholic whose wife or children embraced the reformed doctrine, we have the outline of many family histories in the sixteenth century ; and if we apply the same to any time when old things are passing away and Christian truth is taking to itself new forms, we shall understand how, even among good men, there may be division, how devotion to truth must often involve the straining and perhaps the rupture of the dearest bonds.   If this be so with sincere and kindly people, how much more when the truth encounters blind bigotry, and opposes itself to privileged iniquity, and condemns darling sins, must it raise a tumult in the world.

We do not feel this so keenly.   There is not in our Christianised society the same sharp division ; and in default of tolerance our carelessness suffices to prevent very fierce strife : but still it happens that the truth seems to be anything but a bringer of peace.   Suppose that in a household, nominally Christian, where nevertheless Christian principle has little influence and Christian worship is unknown, some members come under the actual power of godliness and try to let their conduct be as becometh the gospel of Christ, will there not of necessity be difference and even discord ; three going in the broad way and two in the narrow, three loving the world and two trying to serve God ?   Even here and now a man may be called to leave his father and mother, and he must take up his cross and endure hardness for the sake of Christ and the gospel.   " He that endureth unto the end, the same shall be saved."

Of this discord, however, so alien from his spirit and the good news he proclaimed, the word of Jesus is the occasion,—not the cause. Its cause is in the ignorance, the stupidity, the corruption of mankind. His word is a word of peace which bringeth comfort to weary hearts, and, when it has leavened the world, will make wars to cease. But leaven works slowly and silently. It was not his to step forth and cast a spell upon the earth under which the lion should become as the lamb, and rude nations be changed to meekness, and the curse on angry lips turn to a blessing, and the arm raised against a brother become powerless, and the sword drop from the warrior's hand. Not thus doth the kingdom of heaven come. He renews his people in the spirit of their mind, and thus leavens the mass of humanity; and this is of necessity a slow process. Therefore must the disciples, when they were sent out to preach, be warned not to expect that at the sound of their words the strongholds of evil would fall, but to be content to gain a few, and ready to be hated of all men for his name's sake.

It must not be supposed that we wish to defend, or even offer apology for, the strifes which rend the Christian community, when we say that a consideration of what is here advanced should go to moderate somewhat the censure passed upon the followers of Jesus.   For the most part that censure is fully deserved.   Our wars and fightings come from the lusts which war in our members ; and any censure which leads us to be ashamed of those fightings and conquer those lusts, must be accepted as the reproach of a friend.   But it may be noticed that it is not always and entirely to the bad passions of Christians that the proverbial bitterness of religious controversy and cruelty of religious war are to be traced.   It may be the very keenness of their zeal for truth and God, the intense conviction they have of the importance of religion and the danger of error, that makes them so impatient of opposition and so ready to forget the restraints of good temper and Christian charity.   Violence and strife are, however, none the less evil, none the less to be bewailed and avoided.   They are against the law of Christ.   It is on peacemakers that his blessing rests.   His disciples ought to aim at living peaceably with all men, and if they must contend earnestly, to do so without wrath and malice, to be courteous and forbearing, and to rule their spirits, ever remembering that it is by such means that they bear witness for him and let their light shine before men.

Finally, let those who believe in Jesus rest

assured that the sword is only for a while, and hold fast the hope that the good time is coming when peace shall be found upon earth and goodwill prevail among men. When the strife is hottest and the warfare most bloody, when the spirit of division is most active where it should least be found, let them comfort one another with the assurance that this is for a time, and that beyond these voices there is peace.

> " For a' that, an' a' that,
> It's comin' yet, for a' that ;
> That man to man the warld o'er
> Shall brothers be for a' that."

XXXVII.

COVETOUSNESS.

MR. FROUDE, in one of his thoughtful and suggestive *Short Studies*, discussing the cause of the present revival of Romanism, accuses Protestant Christianity of at least passively encouraging the intense pursuit of wealth, which he looks upon as the characteristic feature of modern society. "The clergy," says he, "withdraw into the affairs of the other world, and leave the present world to the men of business and the devil." And he relates how he once ventured to say to a leading Evangelical preacher in London, that he thought the clergy might keep their congregations from forgetting that there was a law, which, if human laws are powerless to approach the disease of society, would in some shape or other enforce itself. This gentleman, he says, "told him very plainly that he did not look on it as a part of his duty. He could not save the world, nor would he try.

His business was to save out of it individual souls by working on their spiritual emotions, and bringing them to what he called the truth. As to what men should do or not do, how they should occupy themselves, how and how far they might enjoy themselves, on what principles they should carry on their daily work—on these and similar subjects he had nothing to say."

It may be permitted to suppose that this confession owes something of its clearness and point to the practised skill of its reporter ; but even making allowance for this, its frankness and insight are remarkable. Evangelicalism in its later stage was never better described : but it is strange that any man should have seen this so distinctly, without perceiving that he was pronouncing his own condemnation. He certainly succeeded in describing only too faithfully the attitude of the church in regard to this matter ; and explained, as Mr. Froude says, why preachers are losing their hold on the more robust intellects.

The world making haste to be rich, and the church leaving it to its own courses, and cultivating other-worldliness—this being the state of things amongst us at present, let us recall what our Master says : " Ye cannot serve God and mammon. Take heed, and beware of covetousness, for a man's life consisteth not in the abundance of the things which he possesseth. Where your treasure is, there will your heart be also." There is not much room for doubt as to the meaning of these words. It may not be altogether easy to expound them in the ears of a fashionable congregation, of which pampered, but withal pleasant and hospitable, rich men are the mainstay; but there they stand, and others beside them which are even worse: "It is easier for a camel to go through the eye of a needle, than for a rich man to enter into the kingdom of God."

This is strong language certainly, but it is obviously intended to be strong; and there is no violence in it, no fanaticism. Jesus was no communist. It is not true that he began his career as a popular enthusiast declaiming against property; that, himself a poor man and sharing the discontentment of his fellows at the unequal distribution of wealth, he came forward as a sort of well-meaning socialist, who could see no good in a rich man, no fault in those who are poor. This is a fancy sketch for which there is no justification. No doubt it is easy to find passages which, quoted separately, seem to bear out such a theory; but the slightest acquaintance with his life and teaching suffices to show that there is no ground for the opinion. It was not at all in this spirit that he spoke of riches. He neither envied rich men, nor treated the possession of property and enjoyment of luxury as crimes. He knew that riches might be worthily won, and wisely spent. He taught that they are a trust committed to men as stewards, and gave directions for their proper use. It was only from the religious point of view he meddled with the subject. Only in so far as they affect a man's spiritual health and conduct have they any importance in his eyes. His "rich" man, in fact, is not a possessor of riches, but a lover of them, a slave of mammon, one who trusts in uncertain riches and not in the living God.

Of such men, however, he speaks with great plainness, as the proverb about the camel and the needle's eye shows. Against the love of riches, and the snares which they spread in a man's path, he raises his solemn and repeated warning. And this is the sum of his counsels: "Ye cannot serve God and mammon." This is what men must know, that they may serve God and be rich, may serve God and be diligent in business, may serve God and enjoy a great many of the pleasant things wealth can command; but that if they serve riches as their slave, become engrossed by them and the delights they purchase, worship those who have them, and give the strength of their manhood to the getting of them, they cannot serve God.

These counsels he addressed to his disciples generally, the great majority of whom were poor men. The covetousness of which he bids us beware is not only that large greed which covets thousands, and adds house to house and field to field, and makes famous misers and speculative millionaires. It is undue love of money, which may display itself in small things, no less offensively than in great; it is the belief that money is the one thing needful, and to make money the chief end of man.

That this spirit is very prevalent in modern society may be said without exaggeration. It is not disapproved or condemned in itself: when it leads a man into dishonest or questionable practices, these are discountenanced, though not so firmly as a strict moralist might desire, and a Christian must demand; the covetousness itself, the love of money which is the root of the evil, is not condemned, but rather stimulated, and by all the judgments and usages of society fostered in measure ever growing. And however the church may be practically powerless in face of this, the word of Jesus remains: "Take heed, and beware of covetousness."

And he annexes to this command a reason which like the command is opposed to prevailing sentiment, "For a man's life consisteth not in the abundance of the things which he possesseth." Would it be very wide of the mark to say that this matter of the abundance of the things which he possesseth is precisely the most important thing in the eyes of most people at present; that, inasmuch as it is the object of their keenest desire and most strenuous endeavour, their life might not inaptly be said to consist therein? It is easy to say that this is all nonsense and fanaticism; but many men that are neither silly nor fanatical have deliberately recorded this as their reading of the signs of the times. At all events, the word of Jesus standeth sure: "A man's life consisteth not in the abundance of the things which he possesseth." Even the world has better things to offer us, things which wealth cannot buy but is more likely to destroy: and there is a higher life to which we are called, in regard to which riches are a source of danger, and covetousness is ruin. Covetousness is idolatry ; it is the prolific source of evil tempers and horrid crimes ; and it is itself an effectual means of banishing God from the thought and life of a man.

Besides his counsel and the reason annexed, Jesus spake a parable which we call that of the "rich fool." It is in the twelfth chapter of Luke's Gospel, and requires no explanation. There is no trace of fanaticism in it at any rate. The example is of the simplest and, so to speak, most innocent kind. The man had not stained his soul with crime. His wealth came from the increase of his land. He did not put it to immoral uses, but only proposed to store it for his own benefit and spend it for his own enjoyment. He only allowed himself to be absorbed by it, to forget God, to puff himself up, to pamper himself, to think only of his senses and forget that there was such a thing as his soul, to live as if this world were all. How like many a rich man whose creed, as Mr. Froude puts it, is "that pleasure is pleasant, and that money will purchase it ;" how true a type of the prevailing tendency of modern life ! And how completely the hollowness of it all is exposed in the single line, " Thou fool, this night thy soul shall be required of thee." It is not only, This night thou shalt die, but Thy soul shall be required of thee by one who has some right in it, and to whom answer must be given.

This is indeed a parable, not only for individuals, but for communities, and above all for nations like our own. We are intoxicated by what is called our marvellous progress, that is to say, by the enormous growth of our commerce, and the accumulation of material wealth ; and we are in danger of forgetting that there are greater things than these, that the nation, too, has a soul, that for it there is a life which consisteth not in the abundance of things possessed, that there are other objects of government than merely to facilitate the production and enjoyment of wealth.

The gospel must not be superseded by the dogmas of political economy. That science may not deserve to be called, as Mr. Froude energetically calls it, " the most barefaced attempt that has yet been openly made on this earth to regulate human society without God or recognition of the moral law :" but it certainly must not be regarded as furnishing a complete rule of life, and ought not without remonstrance to be allowed to " take possession of the air, to penetrate schools and colleges, to control the action of legislatures." Political economy is simply the more or less accurate description of the facts of social life in its various developments, and of the laws which may be formulated from observation of these facts. It takes account chiefly, sometimes solely, of the selfish side of human nature, and treats social organisation from the point of view of pure profit and convenience. It represents men as acting from selfish or prudential considerations, and, inasmuch as the great mass of men do act selfishly and all ought to act prudently, there is a very considerable amount of truth and wisdom in the current maxims of this school. The professors of this "dismal science" have collected a great deal of useful information, have established some valuable principles, and have taught us some truths which deserve more attention than they receive. Their labours do not merit to be lightly spoken of, and from them the disciples of Jesus have very much to learn. They are, in their generation, wiser than we. But, of course, if these gentlemen, instead of promulgating scientific truth or advancing probable opinions, claim that their principles shall exercise an exclusive or dominant influence upon society;

if the public come, as perhaps they are coming, to believe that there are no higher laws than those of political economy to be obeyed, no nobler ends to be attained, no higher ideals to be worshipped ;—then it is time that the church of Christ should do something to assert the principle of her founder; and if her ministers fail so to do, it is well that men like Mr. Froude should reprove them and stir them up to good works, and if need be take up in their stead the prophet's mantle, and prophecy to the people and to their rulers, as he has more than once to excellent purpose done.

XXXVIII.

THE WILLING SPIRIT AND THE WEAK FLESH.

"THE spirit indeed is willing, but the flesh is weak," was the gracious apology made by Jesus for his three disciples in circumstances peculiarly trying to feelings and temper. It has since been used as an apology very often and very thoughtlessly. The "weakness of the flesh" is made to answer for much that is amiss, and serves as an excuse for many sins which might have been avoided with little difficulty. The "willing spirit" is left out of view. But it is a highly important part of this saying. Even with a willing spirit we need to watch and pray lest we fall by reason of weakness of the flesh ; but what if the spirit be unwilling?

Not to enter into psychological niceties, taking the words as they might be understood by Peter, James, and John, the flesh is that part of us which is of the earth earthy, and is subject to physical and natural law; the spirit is that which, bound to the body in many ways, coming into consciousness with it, disappearing as far as this life is concerned when it dies, is nevertheless higher than the body and belongs to the sphere of things which are eternal and divine.

The question of questions is this, On which side does our spirit stand, with God or against Him, willing or unwilling to do right? Does a man really desire to be good and to do good, not with a vague disposition and purposeless inclination, but with deliberate choice and steady endeavour? This is the issue involved in conversion, that, whereas formerly a man was willing to sin, or at least not willing to forsake evil and do righteousness, he becomes fearful of sin and zealous for good. This was what distinguished the disciples, with all their faults, from others in their time—from the Pharisees who hated Jesus and wanted to destroy him, from the multitude who cared little about him and were ready to be stirred up against him, from Judas who had gone away to betray him; that they were faithful at heart and willing to do his will. This is what distinguishes a Christian now from other men, that, whereas some are distinctly hostile to Christ and to the religious life, some too fond of the sort of life which he condemns, some careless about such things, the converted or Christian man wants to live and tries to live so as to please Christ,—forsakes sin, and watches against it, and prays for deliverance from it, and regards the being overtaken in a fault as the worst evil that can befall him.   This, then, is what we must be sure of in the first instance, that we are born again : we need not begin to correct the errors of the flesh till we have got quit of unwillingness of spirit. Blessed are they of whom, amid all their shortcomings, their gracious Master can say that their heart is true and their spirit willing in his sight.

"But the flesh is weak."   Yes, we all know about that.   When the will is present, it is often hard to perform.   The zeal of an apostle is often confined and thwarted by his bodily infirmity.   He cannot fly over land and sea with the good news of God, or speak to as many as he could wish in his brief working day.   Moses has a great deal to say and to do, but is not a good speaker ; Paul's " bodily presence is weak, and his speech contemptible," and he has a " thorn in the flesh " besides, which vexes and hinders him. There are connected with this fleshly existence propensities and passions which are not extinguished when a man is born of the spirit, but remain to be regulated or subdued. Though a man knows that he must not give way to wrath, he may have a quick temper, and there are occasions when anger will arise; he may be willing to flee youthful lusts, but the presence of this will does not extinguish the lusts; he wants to do good, but is hindered by physical sluggishness and natural indolence, by constitutional shyness or dread of ridicule. The disciples were willing to watch with their Master, but their eyes were heavy and they fell asleep.

To this natural weakness of the flesh is added an infirmity induced by indulgence in sin. Such infirmities, like other natural qualities, we inherit from our ancestors. " No man liveth to himself, and no man dieth to himself." One who weakens his constitution by sinful excess, without question may, and in general does, transmit to his posterity a constitutional weakness. Thus does God visit the sins of the fathers upon the third and fourth generation of their children. Of this there cannot now be any doubt; and it should go to make men now living have mercy on those they are the means of bringing into the world.

The most important part, however, of the infirmities directly resulting from misconduct, are those which are caused by our own habits. Instead of strengthening the flesh by rational control and discipline, men give way to its propensities, and establish habits of indulgence. They even go out of their way to teach themselves new and strange desires, and impose artificial weaknesses. They indulge those desires, natural and artificial, till a certain physical condition is set up. Perhaps by this time they begin to see the error of their ways ; but though indulgence has become hateful to the spirit, it is still pleasant, and may even be necessary to the flesh ; and there is heard an exceeding great and bitter cry : " O wretched man that I am, who shall deliver me from the body of this death ?"

From this it appears how it is that we must obey the accompanying counsel : " Watch and pray that ye enter not into temptation." We must first of all take care that our spirits are willing, and not willing only, but vigilant ; not only possessed with a sincere desire to do what is right, but alive to the necessity of carrying

out our purpose, and asserting over the flesh
the needful and rightful sway. And we must
make ourselves acquainted with the weakness
of the flesh and its temptations, that we may
know against what we have especially to guard,
and what measures of precaution or defence it
behoves us to adopt. We must watch intelligently, systematically, and thoroughly. Know
thyself; discipline thyself. Let the principle
of habit, so readily the servant of sin, be made
to minister to that which is pure and lovely
and of good report. So in the weakness of the
flesh may strength be made perfect ; and
virtues, at first cultivated by painful self-denial,
become so easy and familiar, that the difficulty
and the pain would lie in following other ways.

We must also pray for God's blessing and aid.
We need not look for physical or moral
miracles. We cannot hope for the reversal of
the natural ordinances of our being, for the
sudden cessation of carnal desires, for the
absolute eradication of tendencies inherited or
acquired. It is no part of the divine plan of
our education that we should never be tempted
at all. Though the heavenly Father tempteth
no man with any desire or design to work his
· fall, he leadeth us into temptation as every

father has to lead his sons ; and it is thus that he trains us to perfection. We need not, and we should not pray never to be tempted at all. "Not that thou shouldest take them out of the world, but that thou shouldest keep them from the evil." "That ye be strengthened with might by the spirit in the inner man ; so that, being strong in the Lord and in the power of his might, ye may stand." If there is One for whose holiness we may give thanks, One who loves us and yearns over us, and desires to see us brought unto perfection ; if, in a word, there is any truth in the religion of Jesus, this is a rational and even necessary prayer :—

"Almighty God, who dost bid us walk as pilgrims and strangers in this passing world, seeking that abiding city which thou hast prepared for us in heaven ; we pray thee so to govern our hearts by thy Holy Spirit, that we, avoiding all fleshly lusts which war against the soul, and, quietly obedient to the government which thou hast set over us, may show forth thy glory before the world by our good works." Amen.

XXXIX.

THE UNPARDONABLE SIN.

IT is not without reason that Saurin, in his great sermon on the subject of this section, calls it " dark, thorny, and well-nigh impenetrable." But much of its thorniness comes from contact with theological theories, and if we keep clear of them, though it may be thorny and somewhat dark, it may prove neither so impenetrable nor so dangerous as it seems.

There is no doubt that Jesus is reported to have spoken thus : " All manner of sin and blasphemy shall be forgiven unto men ; but the blasphemy against the Holy Ghost shall never be forgiven unto men. And whosoever speaketh a word against the Son of man, it shall be forgiven him, but whosoever speaketh against the Holy Ghost it shall not be forgiven him, neither in this world nor in the world to come." It is true that the words occur in the course of a narrative which gives an account of the healing of a deaf and dumb demoniac, and that in referring to it we may seem to depart from our rule of avoiding matters of doubtful disputation; but we do not require to express any opinion, or to demand any assent, on the questions raised by such narratives, which are well-nigh as thorny as the subject of the unpardonable sin. All that we have to note is, that supposing these words to be correctly reported and set in their original historical connection, taking them as they stand, they furnish no ground for the morbid superstitions to which they have given occasion.

In the first place it is to be observed that they occur in the course of a reply, or, as we might say, a rebuke to the Pharisees, and are to be treated, therefore, not as a calm statement of an abstruse doctrine, but as a warm reproof, administered by one who maintained indeed a seemly dignity, but was strongly moved by the opposition of his adversaries. In the second place it must be observed that there is no mystery here as to what is meant by the sin. Mark tells us plainly that he spake thus, " because they said, He hath an unclean spirit." He recognised in their opposition on that occasion an element of deliberate hostility to the kingdom of heaven, which made it something different from ordinary unbelief in his Messiahship, and warned them that such a sin could not be forgiven ; not on account of any mysterious and arbitrary divine decree, which he does not allege, but because of the deep-seated evil of heart which it disclosed.

In the same way it will be found that this phrase, or one that is equivalent, appears in the Epistles in passages of a warning cast, and is applied to the act of deliberate apostasy from the faith of a Christian.

The unpardonable sin of blasphemy against the Holy Ghost is something definite and determined ; not a certain mysterious transgression as to which God retains in his own hand the right of vengeance which he has resigned as against all other sins and blasphemies, but a distinct offence, whose essence consists in wilful, deliberate, and spiteful opposition to what is known to be highest and best.

It is not to blaspheme against the Holy Spirit to form, concerning religious events, judgments which rest on mistaken opinions concerning his manner of working, or to criticise and oppose what may be a good work, if we do this in ignorance and with a right purpose. If a man sees what he believes to be a work of darkness announced as a work of God, or finds things which can be naturally explained paraded as results of special and miraculous intervention, he is bound to testify for the truth ; he must do so with caution and charity, but he need not be deterred by any superstitious dread of fatal blasphemy. An error of judgment, even a culpable error, a hasty judgment, is not blasphemy,—not that wilful and deliberate opposition to the divine Spirit which drew so strong words from the mouth of the meek Saviour.

It is not apostasy—not the 'drawing back unto perdition'—if a man falls away from the faith for a time, gives way to doubts, or even denies Christ in express terms. His chosen disciples forsook him, and Peter denied with an oath ; and they were forgiven. Wherever there is the possibility of repentance there is room for hope ; and not till a man has come to cherish deliberate hatred to the truth in which he lived and which he still knows to be true, is there any reason to think of the sin which is unto death.

Persons are to be met with occasionally who are oppressed by a melancholy and rooted despair. Reminded of the promises, they say : I know them, but they are not for me. Told that they are for all, they reply : Yes, for all, but not for me, I am an exception to the rule. Reasoned with, that that is to distrust the divine mercy and make God a liar, they admit it, and declare that this is their burden and their fear, that they have been guilty of a blasphemous unbelief, and thus committed the unpardonable sin. It were easy to show, if such persons were at all accessible to reason, that they have done nothing of the kind ; but the truth is, theirs is a case rather for the physician than for the pastor or divine.   Let friends cheer them as well as they may, and commend them to the Father of mercies, asking him to give them a right spirit, and make them hear joy and gladness, that the bones which he hath broken may rejoice.

Again, there are persons quite sane, and undoubtedly pious, who torment themselves unnecessarily on this point. Encouraging mysterious forebodings, and groping among the darker places of Scripture, they begin to say : What if I have committed this sin ? What if some day I should fall into it, and never be forgiven ? Such persons forget that this is a matter which cannot possibly be in doubt. No man can put himself into such a relation to God without knowing it. His dread and horror of

it is a token that he is far from such a state.
There is no "what if" in the case.   His sins
may be many, but if he repents they shall be
forgiven.   There is no such thing in religion
as a mysterious possibility of stumbling unwit-
tingly into the great transgression.   It cannot
be committed except by deliberate choice and
effort.   While, therefore, vigilance is wise and
humility to be commended, excessive and craven
fear is foolish and to be condemned.   No one
who has received the word of Jesus can suffer
himself to be the slave of any such superstition.
Were this single passage more mysterious than
it is, there is enough in the rest of his teaching
to prevent us from listening to counsels of
trouble and unbelieving fear.   No sin is
unpardonable of which a sinner repents.   In
this position we may stand firm, and from it no
unbelief and no sophistry should ever dislodge
us.   "There is joy in heaven over one sinner
that repenteth, more than over ninety and nine
just persons that need no repentance.   This my
son was dead, and is alive again ; and was lost,
but is found."

XL.

JUDGMENTS.

ON the subject of providence the doctrine of
Jesus is plain and simple. He makes no distinction of general and particular providence,
but refers all events to God, who holds the
stars in their courses, and numbers the hairs on
his children's heads.

On the question of what are called special
providential visitations or judgments we have
his verdict in the narrative of his conversation
with those who told him of the Galileans whose
blood Pilate mingled with their sacrifices.
"Suppose ye that these were sinners above all
that dwelt in Jerusalem—or those eighteen
upon whom the tower in Siloam fell? I tell
you, Nay: but, except ye repent, ye shall all
likewise perish."

There is a God who has prepared judgments
for scorners: but all calamities are not judgments; nor is it only the wicked that are the

victims of accident, disease, and war. While, therefore, we keep our minds open to such lessons as God in his providence teacheth, we are not to be too hasty and confident in our reading of the meaning of events. Especially, we must not be too ready to trace the avenging justice of God in the misfortunes which befall our neighbours ; because we are here exposed not only to mistakes of ignorance but to the temptation of judging uncharitably.

The safe rule is to think most of judgments which we can connect with our sins, and regard as manifestly appointed for our correction. This, indeed, is contrary, almost opposite, to the common way, which is to neglect what is frequent and obvious, and to make much of startling calamities. Even as men were apt to suppose that corn grew of its own accord, and the sun rose every day as matter of course, and daily bread came as the natural reward of labour ; whilst they were ready to see the finger of God in the appearance of a comet, the outbreak of a pestilence, or the fall of a tower : so they overlooked those chastisements which were regularly inflicted upon their folly and misdeeds ; and trembled at terrible catastrophes which had no natural connection with them and

their ways.   And it is not only that this was
done in times of darkness and superstition.   As
a rule, people take little account of God when
things are moving in their accustomed course,
but straightway begin to speak of him when
something unusual is interposed.   When Lisbon
was swallowed up by earthquake, or London
desolated by plague, men began to talk of
divine judgment, and to give their various versions of its meaning.   Thousands swear and
blaspheme day after day and nothing happens to
them; but if once in a while a blasphemer drops
down dead with an oath on his lips, the story is
told by the religious press as a judgment of
God.   It would be more to the purpose if,
showing less fondness for exceptional and, to
use a modern word, sensational occurrences, the
public would give more heed to the grand and
useful lessons which are taught by the common
course of divine providence.   When we see an
intemperate man bearing in his body the fruit
of his sin ; when we hear of a filthy village or
town being swept by smallpox or fever ; when
we see a nation which has despised public faith,
and allowed domestic misrule and disorder to
grow unchecked, falling into bankruptcy, rent
by civil discord, or crushed by foreign war ;

these are judgments which we ought to ponder and inwardly digest, for by them we may be made wise and stirred up to reform ourselves, and fight with the evil that is in the world.

So likewise in the smaller, but to every one infinitely important, concerns of private life ; if men would lay to heart daily warnings, note the consequences of actions, trace the results of evil tempers, observe the lessons written in the body after an ill-spent night, they would gather more wisdom than by blundering over curious coincidences and putting narrow interpretations on events whose causes and purposes lie utterly beyond their ken.   We should always, in interpreting divine judgments, endeavour to follow them up to the evils with which they are actually connected, and not sit down to speculate at large on their meaning ; never taking it upon us, especially in the case of other men, to say for what particular sin the visitation is sent, unless there is a manifest, or at least a perceptible, connection between the two.

Upon occasion of any serious calamity, such as epidemic disease, a public fast is sometimes appointed, and Christian people are exhorted to prayer and repentance.   These are never out of place, and it is very right and meet that in time of national calamity we should think of our sins, national and personal. That is a proper use of affliction, against which there is nothing to be said. But when good folks come forward, as they are ready to do on such occasions, to instruct us as to the particular sin or sins for whose chastisement the calamity has been sent —when one sees in it a punishment of national drunkenness, another connects it with the practice of running Sunday trains, another still insists that national luxury is the iniquity specially intended, none of them having any principle to guide him, but each following his own imagination, and fixing on the sin which happens most to engage his attention, we may reasonably decline to be convinced. We do not presume to interpret the will of God except where he has given some plain indication ; and unless we wish to make religion ridiculous we must refuse to encourage such silly attempts to prophesy in his name.

But when physicians show us the causes of disease ; teach us how it is bred in filth, and spread by folly ; when they lead us to regard it not as a miraculous visitation but as the result of the sure working of principles which cannot be violated with impunity ; when they say that the cause of an epidemic is our suffering people to herd like swine in crowded and ill-ventilated rooms, our breathing foul air or drinking polluted water, our being careless about vaccination, our neglecting precautions against infection,—then let those that have ears to hear listen attentively. Let us not care though the philosophers do not say much about God, so long as they discover to us his ways. Let us not be much concerned though, leaving their province, they argue that he has nothing to do with the matter ; but be thankful to them for helping us, as they are doing, to understand the laws which we believe to have been ordained by him.

XLI.

REWARD.

A CERTAIN discrepancy is sometimes felt to exist between the rewards held out in Christian teaching, and that self-denial which is the central principle of Christian life. It is even alleged as an objection against Christianity that it directly encourages a selfish view of religious life. "It declares," so in substance it is said, " that we are to do good in order that we may be rewarded, and to avoid evil lest we should be punished. In this there is nothing that appeals to the nobler feelings of humanity. That the rewards are to be received not now and in earthly shape but afterwards in heaven, makes no real difference. It matters not whether you pay a man with a few coins on the spot or promise to give him a large sum next year. In either case you pay him. Your religion of heavenly rewards is simply a kind of refined self-seeking ; and that is a nobler system which, denying or ignoring immortality, presents to us good and evil as they are in themselves, inviting us to forsake the one because it involves degradation, to cleave to the other because it is becoming and right."

That the charge herein contained holds good as against some forms of Christianity and the type of character which they have fostered may be true. It is not true that it has any real force as against the truth as it is in Jesus. Christian motive is as high and unselfish as those lofty moralists can desire; we are to be perfect as our Father in heaven is perfect, that we may be the children of God. God is the Christian's model and the Christian's reward. This may be transcendental or fantastic; but it cannot be called mean.

There is no doubt that Jesus speaks frankly about reward. The beatitudes are promises of reward; speaking of alms-giving and prayer, the reward of the Father who seeth in secret is opposed to the reward of men; through the whole Sermon on the Mount there runs a reference more or less express to the punishment of transgressors, and the reward of those that do well; and in more than one parable the subject is illustrated. Moreover, reward is a fact to which it would be strange if a teacher of right conduct did not refer. But it by no means follows that his reference to it has a tendency to foster selfishness. On the contrary, we maintain that the very opposite of this is true.

We distinguish between divine rewards and mere prizes. A prize is something promised to excellence, having no necessary connection with the course of conduct by which it is to be gained, but being attached thereto by arbitrary appointment. A book or medal is given to the school-boy who is at the head of his class ; a sum of money or a medal to the exhibitor of the best bullock or machine at a show, or the owner of the fleetest horse on a race-course. This is the common form of human reward ; and if this conception be transferred to the sphere of religion, and it be supposed that Jesus offers dazzling prizes in the kingdom of heaven, there is no wonder that a doubt should be suggested whether that is a good method of elevating and regenerating mankind. We may be allowed, without proof, to say that the rewards of Jesus are not of the " prize " kind.

We distinguish also between material and spiritual reward. If Christian recompense were of a gross nature, if it belonged in any way to the lower or selfish part of our being, if we were invited to walk in the narrow way because thus we should have the least pain, the greatest gratification, there would be cause for regret that no better way than this could be found of redeeming us from vain conduct, that no higher chords—for higher chords there are in the heart of man—had been struck by a Saviour's hand. But if the reward of Jesus is purely spiritual, if he teaches us to deny ourselves, and so find greater fullness of life ; if, lifting us out of ourselves, he directs to the Highest all our thoughts, aspirations, hopes, and purposes,—then, though it cannot but be that the reward of compliance is a great one, it is unjust to say that it is of a low kind, or that it appeals to selfish considerations. As the Psalmist said, " In keeping of thy commandments," not by keeping or for keeping, but "in keeping thy commandments is great reward ;" so does Jesus teach that the reward of godly living is in the perfection of the spiritual life.

In the sixth chapter of the Gospel according to Luke, in the course of what is either a condensed version of the Sermon on the Mount, or a report of a discourse closely similar to it, he says : " Love your enemies, and do good, and lend, hoping for nothing again; and your reward shall be great, and ye shall be the children of the Highest: for he is kind to the unthankful and the evil." Can it be that any heart is so dull or so gross as to read this as an appeal to selfishness in any guise or form? Is it conceivable that, inculcating unselfish kindness with so singular power and beauty, he should spoil his lesson by the mention of a huge bribe, offering, as an inducement to this lofty strain of pure virtue, simply a bigger return than could be expected upon earth, a better investment of our benevolence? Is that a possible, not to say reasonable, reading of an argument of which this is the gist, 'Men can love their friends: God loves his enemies. Men can do good to those who can repay: God is kind to the unthankful and the evil. Be ye like the Highest: let nothing lower content you: be perfect as your Father in heaven is perfect.'

In one of his parables we find, in the sentence put into the mouth of the master who had given the talents to his servants, a formula, as it were, of divine recompense. "Well done, good and faithful servant; thou hast been faithful in a few things, I will make thee ruler over many things: enter thou into the joy of thy Lord."

This is regarded as a flagrant example of a selfish morality, or at least of accommodation to the tastes of a carnal mind. It might be sufficient to point out that this is part of a parable, and is not to be supposed to be carefully adapted in every detail to spiritual things. But one is disposed to waive this, and to challenge that interpretation of the words. Are they so low and grovelling after all ? Taking them, not as part of a parable, but as an anticipation of final award, do they contain a promise of selfish enjoyment ? do they raise visions of a paradise after the fashion of Mahomet's, only more splendid and more pure ? According to this formula the elements of Christian recompense are these :—consciousness of divine approval, promotion in divine service, share in divine joy.

Praise is doubtful, and flattery is vain. The supreme grace of humility is endangered in one who permits himself to care even for good men's praise. It is a good rule of Christian practice not to seek the praise of men, lest we be puffed up in vain conceit. But the approval of such a master as Jesus is a safe and worthy object of ambition, and the praise of God makes no man vain. There is no better ground of rejoicing than the testimony of a man's conscience that in simplicity and godly sincerity he has his conversation in the world. In this consciousness of being right with God, becoming always clearer and deeper, will be the faithful servant's reward throughout eternity. If he receive nothing more, if only he have a good conscience, and hear within him this emphatic "well done," he shall in no wise lose his reward.

Promotion, looked at merely as involving rise in rank and increase of emolument, is doubtless an object of a carnal ambition ; and to carnal minds it is perhaps such things that are suggested by the phrase "being made ruler over many cities." But surely it is only a low and vulgar apprehension that can so read the words of Jesus. He is entitled to expect that those who have sat at his feet should have learned to think more of the honours and responsibilities of high office than of its ornaments, more of work than of pay. If we take his promise as meaning, "I will exalt you to prouder station and make a prince of you, and you shall have a fine palace and crowds of attendants, and men shall call you right honourable or most serene," the fault is our own. Here is another paraphrase, "You have been faithful in a humble employment, I can now entrust to you larger and weightier tasks: I have more and higher work to do, and I put it into your hands." Is not this more in the spirit of Christ? And is not this, which, apart from this passage, is unquestionably part of the idea of Christian recompense, a reward fit to fire the noblest ambition? What higher or purer hope can any one set before himself than thus to abound and increase in the work of the Lord?

Need it be added that the crowning recompense, a share in the joy of the Lord, is something altogether above the sphere of carnal apprehension or selfish desire. Into this joy the follower of Christ enters here and now, in measure as he receives the master's spirit. But his spirit is the spirit of self-sacrifice, and his joy the joy of doing good. Is it not known that it is in this way that a man tastes the purest and most lasting joy in this world; that true happiness eludes the grasp of those who make it the object of their direct endeavour, and is found unsought by those who go out of themselves to make others happy, upon whom cometh the blessing of him that was ready to perish, and who cause the widow's heart to sing for joy? "He is the happiest of men who has most room in his heart, and he most blessed who blesses most, even as God who blesses all is blessed above all."[1]   The joy of Christ is great above all measure, because he sees of the travail of his soul and is satisfied, because he lives in perfect love : when, being made perfect through suffering, we enter into his love, then shall his joy also remain in us, and our joy shall be full.

[1] Robertson's *Pastoral Counsels*, p. 50.

NOTE.

SINCE the foregoing remarks left my hands, I have read Mr. Stopford Brooke's recently published volume, " *The Fight of Faith.*"   The Sermon on " Sacrifice and Reward," therein contained, must already be well known to many ; and to them the argument here presented, though I hope it may have approved itself to their judgment, will not be entirely new.   On several points, indeed, but particularly on this of reward, Mr. Brooke has somewhat anticipated me.   I have thought it best, however, to let my remarks stand as they were originally written.   And I embrace the opportunity of expressing my high admiration of his book, and of particularly recommending to those of my readers who do not already know it, a study of that sermon, in which, among other things that cannot fail to interest and edify, they will find some of my opinions enforced with a power and eloquence to which I lay no claim.

XLII.

ETERNAL LIFE.

JESUS does not attempt to prove the immortality of the soul. He assumes it. With the exception of the Sadducees all his hearers believed in it, and he could take it for granted, along with the other fundamentals of religion and morality. What is distinctive of his doctrine is, that he speaks chiefly of eternal life, which is not with him present life indefinitely prolonged, as some think, but a higher life than the earthly and sensuous, the life of a regenerated spirit, the life of love, the life hid in God, one of whose characteristics of course is that it can never end. Eternal life implies immortality, but is something infinitely more.

On one occasion, being drawn by the Sadducees into a discussion on the subject of a resurrection, and having evaded an ingenious quibble with which they tried to puzzle him, he attacked their unbelief in these words : " Now that the dead are raised, even Moses showed at the bush, when he called the LORD the God of Abraham and of Isaac and of Jacob: for he is not a God of the dead, but of the living." It may be suspected that many think this little better than a quibble, and wonder why his opponents did not retort that when Moses gave Jehovah this name he indicated no more than that he was the same being whom the patriarchs had worshipped in their day. It must, therefore, be observed that this is not intended as a direct enunciation of the doctrine of resurrection, such a proof-text as, for example, the first verse of the fifth chapter of the Epistle to the Romans is of the doctrine of justification by faith. It is admitted that no such proof-text can be found; that was known to Pharisees as well as Sadducees; and Jesus did not profess to have discovered something which had escaped the eyes of so many scribes and scholars poring over every letter of the sacred text so long and so carefully. Speaking to Sadducees who stood by the Pentateuch, he says that the doctrine in question is really involved in the name of God, since God is not the God of the dead but of the living. And this is no verbal argument: as such, it would have been, as has been hinted above, a very poor one, which could have aston-ished only an ignorant multitude, and would hardly have silenced the Sadducees. The argu-ment turns not on the words but on the relation expressed in the name. God would not have called himself their God if they were not alive. He would, to adapt the language of the Epistle to the Hebrews, have been ashamed to call himself their God if he had not prepared for them a city. "Shall God," says George Mac-donald, in the best exposition of this verse I have met with, "call himself the God of the dead, of those who were once alive, but whom he could not or would not keep alive? Is that the Godhood in its relation to those who worship it? The changeless God of an ever-born and ever-perishing torrent of life, of which each cries with burning heart, 'My God,' and straightway passes into the godless cold." So far from being a verbal argument, this is one which places the faith of immortality on its best and deepest foundation, on the nature of God the Eternal, and our relation to him.

Among the natural arguments for a future life, a favourite one is drawn from a considera-tion of the nobility of human nature and the greatness of its achievements. 'How grand a creature is man! How wide his faculty! How splendid the performance of his genius! How high his aspirations! his thoughts, how they wander through eternity! Is it credible that such a being should vanish into nothing?' But there is another side to the shield. It is not to be denied that man's physical structure is closely allied to that of the beasts that perish. Generation after generation, with all their talents affections, and aspirations, have passed away, and no whisper from one of them has broken the silence of the buried past. And it must be remembered that man is not all the noble creature thus described. With even more obvious truth it may be said, 'What a miserable wretch is man! How vile his heart! How cruel his passions! How monstrous his vices! How grovelling his desires!' "There are," says one who was no misanthrope or unbeliever,— Robertson of Brighton, "days and hours when it seems to us almost incredible that such things as we are should live again at all."

But the security which is sought in vain in ourselves may be found in God and in our relation to him. Let there be introduced into that argument the idea of a wise and good God, whose Fatherly will rules all things; let it be

granted that our souls and bodies are his work-
manship, that we are his offspring ; and it may
be argued with some force that it is impossible
that we can perish. The eternity and un-
changeableness of God is, to those who call him
Father, a sure pledge of their own immortality ;
because he lives they shall live also, for all live
in him.

It is abundantly evident that atheism and
denial of immortality go together. Banish from
this wondrous universe the God who made it
and keeps it ; believe in nothing which your
hands cannot feel or your mathematics analyse ;
reduce thought to a change in brain-tissue, and
affection to a nervous thrill ; say with ancient
Sadducees and modern materialists that there
is neither angel nor spirit,—and you get rid of
the very idea of a future state, and of all the
hopes and all the terrors with which it has so
long been associated in the minds of mankind.
It is equally certain that a firm faith in God,
such as those have who believe the word of
Jesus, carries with it the assurance of immortality. To one who knows the true God, and lives
in his love, it is monstrous to suppose that the
saints of God have passed away as if their lives
had been no more than bubbles on the stream

of being. There are moral and spiritual contradictions which it is as hard for a spiritually-minded person to receive as it is for intellectual men to entertain those that are of a logical kind. Such a contradiction, a hopeless moral absurdity, it is to say that Jesus of Nazareth passed away for ever on Calvary, and that those who have fallen asleep in him have perished. That, having led a life like his, and exhibited for a few short years a character so lofty, so pure, so winning, he should be annihilated; that having spoken as he did about his Father in heaven, and worked and suffered in such open consciousness of his presence and unbounded confidence that he was going to him, Jesus found at the last that he had been building on the sand, and, bowing his head on the cross with the thought of the Father in his heart, passed out into nonenity as the millions had done before; that Stephen, saying with his last breath, "Lord Jesus, receive my spirit," spoke to an empty void which was about to swallow him up, as it had swallowed the Lord on whom he called; that Paul's life rested on a lie and ended in a disappointment; that the loved and honoured dead, whose memory is so dear and sacred, have found no resting-place, but sunk into a godless abyss, never to rise again ;—these are contradictions, difficulties of unbelief, beside which the difficulties of belief, though they are neither few nor small, seem to the heart, with which man believeth, not worthy to be named. This is not, as some allege, to believe in a future life because we wish it ; it is that in view of the whole case we cannot otherwise believe.

So also is it absurd to tell a man, who is already conscious of being an heir of that eternal life of which Jesus speaks, that he is to be snuffed out like the flame of a candle, and to have no other destiny than such as awaits the other constituents of the soil with which his dust must mingle. The felt presence of the spirit is, as St. Paul justly says, an earnest of what shall be ; and the life of sonship is one over which death can have no power. For one whose heart is full of the ideas of Jesus, and whose life is full of the works that the love of Jesus inspires, who knows that he is making progress in holiness, and has the witness of spiritual experience that he is a son of God— for such an one the problem of the future is solved ; the question is not one of survivance ; he is persuaded " that neither death nor life, nor angels, nor principalities, nor powers, nor things present, nor things to come, nor life, nor death, nor any other creature, shall be able to separate him from the love of God which is in Christ Jesus our Lord."

XLIII.

THE EXAMPLE OF JESUS.

IT is not essential for the reception of moral and religious teaching that the teacher himself should be perfect in conduct. That is to say, a bad man may give good advice, and if we discern the wisdom of the counsel, it would be foolish to neglect it on account of imperfection in the character of the counsellor. But, undoubtedly, the better the teacher's own life is the more likely he will be to persuade men to accept his doctrines ; and there are some truths which we should scarcely like to hear from a bad man, others which we could hardly bear to receive without the encouragement of a great example. It is a good thing for those who have to set forth the claims of the doctrine of Jesus that they can so confidently appeal to the records of his life.

More than this, however, has to be said. His words are, in a peculiar manner, bound up with his personality. It is, indeed, impossible to separate them from his life, or truly to understand them apart from his character and deeds. Therefore, although we do not purpose to relate the life of Jesus, we cannot close these remarks on his teaching without referring to the illustration it derives from the life. Perhaps the most valuable portion of his legacy of doctrine is in the brief fragmentary touches of the evangelists which to patient study reveal the greatness and beauty of his example. "The life is the light of men."

Let it be observed that the study of the history of Jesus can be of no use in this respect unless the reality of his manhood is distinctly apprehended. As long as we allow our belief in his divinity to swallow up, as it does with many, the idea of his true humanity ; as long as, in spite of statements about "taking unto himself a true body and a reasonable soul," we fail to realise that he was made in all things like ourselves ; as long as, because we offer him worship, we fail to realise that he was partaker of our infirmities ; as long as to us "being found in fashion as a man" means that his life was not a genuine life, but only a performance in human character by a divine being ; so long must his example be lacking in real interest and power. We must admit no conception of Godhead which in any way interferes with the utter genuineness of his manhood. It is as much against true orthodoxy to disbelieve in his humanity as in his divinity. Godhead, besides, is and must remain a mystery ; but there need be no mystery about the human life, with which we have to do. If we regard it as a true life, differing from ours mainly in this, that it was what a human life ought to be, we may the better receive his word, and strive hopefully to attain to that pureness, sweetness, and active goodness, that perfection which it was the end of his coming to show to us, and enable us to share.

It is obvious how much his teaching concerning the Father is supported and illustrated by his life ; not only because of that community which entitled him to say, " He that hath seen me hath seen the Father," but because of the transparent trustfulness of his own piety, the manifest love he bore to the unseen Father, the resignation he exhibited in agony and death. Thus he teaches, as no mere words could ever have done, to believe how gracious is his Father and our Father, and to obey the first and great commandment.

So also with the second, " Thou shalt love thy neighbour." It is true that we learn a great deal from the parable of the Good Samaritan; but we learn more from the actual conduct of Jesus. We learn what love really is, and what is true sympathy, at once holy and tender, large and fine. We see how this new affection is independent of ties of kindred, and claims of amiability, and hopes of return ; how it cares for the soul without despising the body, and shrinks not from the last sacrifice for the sake of others ; how it has power to win confidence and bestow actual strength. We have further the best answer in the Lord's own practice to a question which we felt bound to consider in a former chapter, Whether the things which he commands are practicable? It was much that he should say to his disciples, "A new commandment I give unto you, that ye love one another ;" but what a wealth of added meaning was in the words, "as I have loved you."

It is, indeed, by the life, imperfectly as it has been apprehended, more than by his doctrine, by what he was more than by what he said, that the law of Christ has been stamped so deeply upon the consciousness of mankind. It was well to say, "Let a man deny himself;" "He that saveth his life shall lose it ; he that loseth his life shall save it." These things are true, and nothing can discredit them. Selfishness can never be good ; sacrifice must always be highest and best. So that as a principle, an impersonal and independent truth, this deserves the assent and obedience of mankind. But it was better when he could say, " Let a man deny himself, and come after me." Unquestionably the great paradox of sacrifice derives much of its power over the hearts of men from the memory of his devoted life, and its association with the cross of Calvary.

The subject of forgiveness may be instanced as one which gains much from a study of his example. It seems a simple matter ; it is, however, anything but simple. It is easy enough in appearance, and even in reality as long as you keep merely on the surface ; but it is not easy either to believe in free pardon of our own sins, or to extend to others that full and salutary forgiveness which Jesus enjoins. The history of religion, with its systems of sacrifice, and penance, and service, and its theories of atonement, sufficiently shows how hard it is for men to receive such a doctrine of forgiveness as he taught. Common experience demonstrates the difficulty of exercising forgiveness, of reconciling the free pardon of sin with a true appreciation of its evil; of uniting a proper resentment and just indignation against wrong, with tolerance and readiness to restore them that are penitent; of steering safely between the indifference of a man of the world, and the rigidity of a fanatic; of so treating offenders that they shall be filled with regret and utter loathing of sin, and at the same time be lifted up and established in a new respect for themselves and a hopeful resolution of amendment.   Parents know that there is nothing more important in the training of children than the exercise of their prerogative of mercy in such a way as to combine strictness and tenderness, to be firm without repelling by hardness, and lenient without seeming to make light of sin.   There is no more weighty function of society than that of binding and loosing, its forgiveness of some sins, and its pitiless exaction of the penalty for others; and not even those who are most willing to be content with things as they are, can deny that there is room for anxious thought and endeavour in this direction.   Statesmen, too, and all who are interested in the treatment of criminals, know well that now, since we are agreed that there are other things to be done with them than to punish them or put them out of the way, there are few more interesting problems than those which are connected with the exercise of a wise and healing mercy. On these and similar delicate points of policy and casuistry, which can only be indicated here, much light may be had from a study of the relation of Jesus to publicans and sinners—his treatment, for instance, of Zacchæus and the woman taken in adultery; in which is to be seen at work a forgiveness which goes deeper than the remission of penalty,—goes, indeed, to the very root of things, and works with sure and salutary influence in the hearts of men.

In like manner the whole subject of meekness and gentleness, of poverty of spirit, of humility, is intimately connected with the example of Jesus. Speaking of these graces we require to combat the suspicion which attaches to them of being scarcely so admirable as the gospels imply; to show that the poor in spirit are not poor-spirited in the lower sense, nor the meek cowardly, nor the humble servile ; to repudiate the tacit assumption that in order to hold his own in the world, and gain the respect of his fellows, a Christian must take all that is said

about meekness and forgiveness with a considerable deduction. This, doubtless, it is possible
to do satisfactorily enough by process of statement and argument : but the shortest and best
way to set such doubts and cavils at rest is to
refer to the man Christ Jesus himself, and see
how the presence of the gentler virtues in such
measure as almost to constitute a characteristic
feature, in no way interfered with a capacity for
indignation and stern rebuke, for bold and crush-
ing argument. There was no want of manliness.
or even of majesty in the meek and lowly Jesus.
He showed a courage which nothing could
daunt, a force of character which gave him
unquestioned ascendency over his neighbours,
and invested him with a natural royalty, and
made him a tower of strength on whom strong
men were fain to lean. So finely, indeed, were
all his qualities blended into a rounded and
complete humanity, that the softest of women
and the firmest of men may equally find an
example in him. In a larger sense than the
Messianic he is the Son of man ; and wide and
profound as are the principles of his doctrine,
there is no part of it which is not illustrated by
his life.

XLIV.

CONCLUSION.

IF it had been the purpose of this book to give
an exhaustive exposition of the words of the Lord
Jesus, it would not have been nearly finished.
When we recall such familiar sayings as that
about little children and the kingdom of heaven;
such parables in a sentence as the " new wine in
new skins," " the mote and the beam," " straining at gnats and swallowing camels ;" such
weighty words as these, " The light of the body
is the eye.   If the light that is in thee be darkness, how great is that darkness ?" " He who
saveth his life shall lose it," " Not till seven times
(must a brother be forgiven), but till seventy
times seven"—when these and other sayings
crowd upon the memory and invite consideration, it is apparent how much and how rich
material for comment yet remains.   But enough
has been said for the present purpose.   It has
not been sought to offer a complete discussion

of the religion of Christ, or attempted to reduce it to a coherent logical scheme; but some of its more salient features have been exhibited, and an endeavour has been made to vindicate it against the assaults of hostile critics and the more dangerous perversions of unwise friends.

If nothing more had been done it would still be something to have called attention to the actual teaching of Jesus; for, strange as the remark may seem, after all that has been said and written in recent times on the subject of the origins of the Christian religion, it is doubtful whether many who reject it are really qualified by knowledge of the fundamental data to form an opinion. It is some time since Archdeacon Hare pointed out that "one proof of the gospel being the most perfect body of moral and spiritual truth ever uttered upon earth, is that the moral truths after which the wise of this world pant, and of which, if they catch a glimpse, they cry εὕρηκα, and bless their genius, and spread their peacock's tail to the sun, are common household words in the New Testament." The remark applies to later writers even more fitly than to those whom he had in view. I remember, for example, to have read, I think in a very fascinating and in many respects admirable book on the

French Humourists by Mr. Besant, after a rather elaborate and bitter paragraph upon priests and clergymen and their manifold sins, a remark to the effect that it is time that we learned that the great thing is personal holiness, and that nothing else will do. Might it not have occurred to the writer that Jesus of Nazareth had enunciated this principle with some plainness and power eighteen centuries ago, and that, with all their shortcomings, his ministers have done something to establish it in the world? Here is another example of this "peacock tail" practice from one of Büchner's books. Having, with a wave of the hand worthy of Mr. Arnold's Zeitgeist himself, brushed aside all existing forms of religion, that clever exponent of materialistic atheism has the coolness to announce this great discovery, " that reciprocity is henceforward to be recognised as the basis of morals, and all religion to be summed up in this; 'Do unto others as ye would that men should do unto you!'"

Is it too much to ask, in view of such things, that before Christianity be vilified or discarded, its Founder's actual teaching shall be studied and fairly judged?

I have not shrunk from confessing that much

error has, in the course of centuries, mingled with his pure doctrine, and that he is more seriously misrepresented by his followers than by opponents: I even insist that he is not to be held responsible for the superstitions of Rome or the dogmatism of Geneva, and desire that in these times of trial we should stand on the foundation Jesus himself has laid. It is an inevitable consequence of the influx of critical ideas into a country hitherto so unhistorical and dogmatic in its religious thought as our own, that the faith of many should be rudely shaken. They find that the evidences on which they were taught to accept Christianity are themselves hard to prove; and they are tempted to throw aside Christianity itself as false and vain. They find that the Bible is not the absolutely inspired and infallible Book they once supposed; and they cast it aside as a tissue of old wives' fables. Scholastic dogmas, which to them used to represent religious truth, give way under the powerful solvent of criticism; and they think they must abjure religion altogether. The purely negative method of Strauss, now out of date in his own country, and yielding to the equally bold and trenchant, but reverent and constructive, criticism of Ewald or Keim, is still, to many amongst us, as the revelation of a new world of thought; and chiming in as it does with the prevalent agnosticism of our native scientific school, is supposed to have settled the religious question once for all. And so it is common to have it quietly assumed that Christianity is effete and dying; or even to hear it said that it is a degrading superstition from which the Zeitgeist and his literary and scientific lieutenants are rapidly delivering this enlightened generation. I ask ingenuous inquirers to pause before they accept such sweeping verdicts, and to believe that there is something in Christianity which will endure after all this sifting; to consider whether there may not exist ground for a comfortable faith independent of doubtful details and forms that are perishing; to consider also, which is more important, whether there is not here plainly presented to us a claim for obedience and for homage, not of the panegyrical or liturgical kind, but of sincere aspiration and steadfast endeavour.

More directly the argument advanced in favour of the religion of Jesus in its original form shall not be pressed here. If readers do not draw for themselves the conclusions desired,

it would avail little to set them down in logical
form, and less to trick them out in a rhetorical
peroration.   One thing has to be said, that although in the foregoing pages no parade has been
made of critical discussion, some care has been
taken to build on sure ground, to make use of
materials which sound and even severe scholar-
ship has approved ; that no theory has been assumed on the subject of inspiration, no use made
of the evidence of miracles, no advantage taken
of the Master's personal claims ; and that thus
a case has been adduced in which the freest of
thinkers, whose mind is in the fairest suspense
of judgment on many matters now in dispute,
may be asked whether there is not in this
teaching something worthy of acceptation,—
whether he who uttered it has not, on this
ground alone, a better claim than any luminary
that has yet appeared, to be called "the Light
of the World."

It may be good also for those who cling
most fondly to traditional forms, to receive
more simply and to study more closely the
truth "as it is in Jesus."   Many old supports
of faith seem to be shaking ; and even believers
will have most light and comfort when they feel
that they are resting on the true foundation,

and have within themselves a witness which
cannot fail. Wherefore let us know the truth,
and the truth shall make us free. " Wait on
the LORD : be of good courage, and he shall
strengthen thine heart." " These things have I
written unto you that believe on the name of
the Son of God ; that ye may know that ye
have eternal life, and that ye may believe on
the name of the Son of God."

FINIS.

Printed by R. & R. CLARK, *Edinburgh.*